DANCE DIVAS

Two to Tango

DANCE DIVAS

Showtime!

Two to Tango

Let's Rock!
(coming soon)

DANCE DIVAS
Two to Tango

Sheryl Berk

BLOOMSBURY
NEW YORK   LONDON   NEW DELHI   SYDNEY

First published in the United States of America in February 2014
by Bloomsbury Children's Books
www.bloomsbury.com

For information about permission to reproduce selections from this book, write to
Permissions, Bloomsbury Children's Books, 1385 Broadway, New York, New York 10018
Bloomsbury books may be purchased for business or promotional use. For information on
bulk purchases please contact Macmillan Corporate and Premium Sales Department at
specialmarkets@macmillan.com

Library of Congress Cataloging-in-Publication Data
Berk, Sheryl.
Two to tango / Sheryl Berk.
     pages   cm.   — (Dance divas ; #2)
Summary: When Miss Toni decides that rivals Liberty and Rochelle will both
perform duets with Hayden in the next competition, the two girls develop
their first crushes on one of the cutest twelve-year-olds in town.
ISBN 978-1-61963-188-5 (paperback) • ISBN 978-1-61963-187-8 (hardcover)
ISBN 978-1-61963-189-2 (e-book)
[1. Interpersonal relations—Fiction. 2. Dance teams—Fiction. 3. Dance—Fiction.] I. Title.
     PZ7.B45236Two 2014   [Fic]—dc23   2013036200

Book design by Donna Mark
Typeset by Westchester Book Composition
Printed and bound in the U.S.A. by Thomson-Shore Inc., Dexter, Michigan
2 4 6 8 10 9 7 5 3 1 (paperback)
2 4 6 8 10 9 7 5 3 1 (hardcover)

To Gaga, aka my mom,
Judy Kahn,
for always believing in me.
Love you muchly

Table of Contents

DANCE DIVAS
Two to Tango

CHAPTER 1

A Star Is Born

Rochelle Hayes jolted up in bed the second her radio alarm clock began blasting.

She sprung out of her covers and danced around, singing into an imaginary microphone. It was 6:00 a.m. on a Saturday morning—hours before she usually had to get up for class at Dance Divas Studio.

Most weekends she dragged her heels and her mom practically had to wave a plate of chocolate chip waffles under her nose to coax her up.

But today was different. Miss Toni, her dance team coach, had specifically asked her to come to the studio at 7:00 a.m. to discuss a new routine she had choreographed *especially* for Rochelle.

"I have a surprise for you, Rochelle," she said, pulling her aside in class one day.

"A surprise?" Rochelle knew in Toni terms that could be a good thing . . . or a bad thing. Or a totally crazy thing.

Antoinette Moore was one of the toughest dance teachers in New Jersey with a reputation that followed her all over the country, wherever she took her team to compete. Toni liked to spring things on Rochelle and her teammates.

Only a few months ago, she'd had the five of them perform a patriotic routine, where she painted their faces to look like the American flag. Rochelle got the worst of it: her face was sprinkled with blue stars. The rest of the girls had red stripes on their cheeks and forehead.

"I look like a Smurf with chicken pox!" Rochelle moaned to her BFF and Divas teammate, Scarlett Borden.

"And I look like the Cat in the Hat's hat!" Scarlett chuckled. "Just go with it!"

Rochelle could always count on Scarlett to calm her down and cheer her up. She was the team's unofficial captain and voice of reason—no matter what Toni had them do.

"I have a dance that I think you'll like . . . for a change," Toni had said to Rochelle.

"Is it hip-hop?" Rochelle asked excitedly. "Do I get to bust a move at Leaps and Bounds?" The competition was one of the coolest and fiercest in the country, and the girls were looking forward to the trip to Delaware in a week.

Toni shook her head. "No, it's not hip-hop. But it's colorful."

Rochelle suddenly had visions of herself dressed like a rainbow . . . or a clown . . . or a confetti birthday cake.

"What do you mean by *colorful?*" she asked nervously.

"Trust me, it's a sizzling hot number," Toni replied.

So that's it, Rochelle thought to herself. *She's going to make me dress like a giant strip of bacon!*

"I am not saying anything more until Saturday morning," Toni insisted. "Be here at 7:00 a.m. sharp, ready to work." She tossed her a long flowing orange skirt with tiers of ruffles. "And wear this with your leotard for rehearsal."

Rochelle made a face.

"No arguing." Toni cut her off with a wave of her hand before she had a chance to protest. "This is the most dynamic dance I have ever choreographed, and I think you're the girl to do it."

Back in the dressing room with her fellow Dance Divas, Rochelle was proud but also puzzled. Toni's clues were impossible to decipher. She held up the skirt: "This is what I'm supposed to wear."

"It's not bad," said Scarlett. "It could be worse. Remember that 'Footprints in the Sand' duet we had to do last year?"

Rochelle flinched at the memory. "That sandpaper skirt was so lame!" she said. "Not to mention itchy!"

"The orange color is nice," Bria Chang chimed in. "It reminds me of a sunrise."

Liberty Montgomery wrinkled her nose. "Ruffles? Seriously? That is *so* yesterday . . . not Leaps and Bounds."

Rochelle hated to ever admit Liberty was right, but in this case she had to agree. The ruffles were pretty tacky. She pulled the skirt over her hips and twirled.

"How do I look?" she asked the girls.

Gracie, Scarlett's seven-year-old sister and the youngest Diva, clapped her hands. "You look pazy."

Gracie had a knack for combining words into her own Gracie language. "Pazy" was pretty and crazy rolled up into one.

"You look like a pirate queen, Rock!" she added.

"Arrrr!" Rochelle growled at her. "Ahoy there, mateys! Maybe Toni will have me dance in a peg leg?" She limped around the dressing room. "Eat your heart out, Captain Jack Sparrow!"

Scarlett laughed. "What else did Toni say?"

Rochelle tried to remember her exact words. "Something about this being her most dynamic dance?"

"Maybe you're a superhero? Superheroes are dynamic," Bria suggested. "That would be cool."

Liberty smirked. "You look more like a tangerine than Wonder Woman."

"Liberty . . . ," Scarlett said, trying to referee before a fight broke out. "What happened to Dance Divas stick together—not torture each other?"

"I know! I know! You're Super Citrus!" Liberty cracked up. "The Fantastic Fruit Salad!"

Rochelle inched closer to Liberty, till they were nose-to-nose. "Do you want to say that again?" she dared her.

"Aw, somebody's a little sour." Liberty laughed. "*Orange* you liking my jokes?"

Scarlett held Rochelle back. "It's not worth it, Rock. If Miss Toni hears you guys arguing, she'll take your solo away."

Rochelle took a deep breath and smiled. "That's

really funny, Liberty. You're a riot! I guess you'll have a lot of time to come up with more jokes since you don't have a solo to learn this week."

Liberty stopped laughing. Rochelle had definitely hit a nerve. She knew Liberty was just jealous that Miss Toni hadn't chosen her for whatever special routine she was choreographing.

"Like I care," Liberty tossed back. "I have to go shopping for a dress this weekend with my mom— something really glam to wear to the Grammy Awards."

"That's so nice of your mom!" Bria said innocently. "She's flying back from L.A. just to take you shopping?"

Liberty shot her a look. She'd forgotten that she told Bria her mother was choreographing a music video in Hollywood all week.

"Well, if she has time, she'll come home . . . ," Liberty said, trying to cover.

She grabbed her dance bag and left the dressing room in a huff.

"Wow, Liberty is really upset that you have

Miss Toni's attention this week," Scarlett told Rochelle. "You know how she gets."

Did she ever! But after several months, Rochelle had figured out that Liberty was all bark and no bite. Having a big-time Hollywood choreographer for a mother wasn't easy, and Liberty always wanted to please her—no matter what it took.

"I wish I knew why Miss Toni picked me," Rochelle said.

"Why? Because you're awesome!" Scarlett insisted. "Liberty can do a gazillion *fouetté* turns, but she doesn't have your passion. When you dance, you take people's breath away! You're on fire!"

"Thanks," Rochelle said modestly. "Let's hope Toni thinks so on Saturday."

CHAPTER 2

I Gotta Be Me

"You need a ride, honey?" Rochelle's mom called into her bedroom. She was juggling Rochelle's baby brother, Dylan, on one hip. "I can get my keys and drive you to the studio. Just give me a sec to change Dilly's diaper . . ."

Usually, Rochelle would have welcomed the lift to the studio instead of biking the fifteen blocks. But today, she had so much energy, a bike ride sounded like a good warm-up for whatever Miss Toni had in store.

"I'm a big girl; I can bike it," she said, tickling Dylan's toes.

"Really? No grumping? No, 'Why do I have to get up so early for dance class?'" her mother remarked. "Did aliens come down and take my daughter and replace her with another kid?" She looked in Rochelle's ear. "Hello? Is Rochelle Hayes in there?"

Rochelle giggled. "I'm just excited for this new solo," she explained. "Miss Toni picked me, Mom. *Me*."

"Well, of course she did!" her mother said. "Rock, you're an amazing dancer. It's about time Miss Toni started treating you like the star you are."

Rochelle's parents always told her what a talented dancer she was, but it wasn't very often that her teacher paid her a compliment. Usually, all she got was, "Why are you not doing the choreography I gave you?" or "Rochelle, you can't go out onstage and do whatever you want!"

Rochelle couldn't help it. Sometimes her feet had a mind of their own. When the music began to play, she didn't just hear it, she actually *felt* it.

And it took her places that didn't always fit in with Miss Toni's vision for the routine. To her teacher, that was disrespectful. But to Rochelle, it was simply what dancing was all about: the freedom to express yourself without a care in the world. Whatever emotion she was feeling, she could dance it out.

It had always been this way, for as long as she could remember. When she was five years old, her next-door neighbor and best friend, Kayla, moved all the way to Kentucky. Instead of sitting on her front porch crying, Rochelle ran to her bedroom, blasted a *Disney Princess* CD, and twirled around the room until she was dizzy. She danced to *Cinderella*'s "A Dream Is a Wish Your Heart Makes." The lyrics spoke to her. It didn't bring Kayla back, but it made her feel just a little bit better to move her arms and legs in an expression of her broken heart.

Since Miss Toni had been a dancer her whole life, Rochelle knew she understood this. But the two of them always butted heads. Miss Toni wanted her to wear toe shoes when she preferred to dance barefoot. Toni expected her to spend hours at the *barre* practicing boring positions when Rochelle wanted to leap and spin through the air.

"You cannot be a great dancer without foundation," Toni insisted. "Technique is everything." But Rochelle was convinced that great dancers were born, not made. She wanted to fly across the studio floor while her dance coach made her take baby steps.

It was no secret among the Divas that Rochelle liked to dance to her own beat. She had a reputation for being a bit of a rebel. Scarlett was always afraid that one day she'd push Toni too far—and she'd kick her off the competition team. One time, she came pretty close. A day before the Movin' Up competition in Indiana, Rochelle decided to "redesign" her costume so it would be more comfy.

"You like?" she asked her teammates, modeling an astronaut costume she'd cut off at the legs.

"Oh, boy." Bria gulped. "You chopped off the whole bottom of the costume."

"Not the *whole* bottom," Rochelle insisted. "Just the big balloony legs so I can move better."

"But Rock, Toni had these costumes made to look exactly like space suits," Scarlett reminded her. "She's not gonna be happy you changed her design."

Scarlett was right. The moment Rochelle walked in the studio—without the legs of her space suit—Toni flipped.

"You're supposed to be walking on the moon!" the dance coach shrieked. "You can't walk on the moon in booty shorts!"

"I couldn't dance in that big, bulky space suit," Rochelle insisted. "I felt like a giant marshmallow."

"That was the point!" Toni bellowed. "The authenticity of the struggle! Do you think it was easy for men to walk on the moon?"

Luckily, it was too late to restage the routine. Toni told all the Divas to wear silver shorts and crop tops instead. But as punishment, Rochelle had to wear an astronaut bubble helmet and sit on top of the moon, waving an American flag.

"I feel like I'm inside a fishbowl," she moaned.

"Serves you right," Liberty said. "Too bad Toni didn't make you dress like the man in the moon and wear Swiss cheese."

Scarlett tried to sympathize. "Sorry, Rock. But you knew Miss Toni would go ballistic."

"I can't help it," Rochelle confided in her BFF. "I just have to be me."

She hoped that Toni would one day give up, give in, and stop trying to change her.

Maybe today was the day.

CHAPTER 3

Studio Surprise

When she arrived at the studio, the door was open but the front lobby and hallways were quiet and dark. Dance Divas was usually abuzz with activity and dancers rushing to classes, but it was too early for any of them to begin. She tiptoed toward studio 2, where Miss Toni told her to meet.

The shades were pulled over the studio windows, so Rochelle couldn't see in. But she could hear Miss Toni's voice booming. "And one, and two, and shoulders back, straight knees!"

She pushed the door open slowly and saw a blond bun at the *barre* . . .

Liberty!

"Glad you could join us, Rochelle," Toni called. "Come in. Warm up. Let's get to work."

Rochelle froze in her tracks. "What's she doing here?" she began. "You said this was my dance, *my* solo."

"I never said I was giving you a solo. In fact, I was envisioning a duet," Toni explained.

"No way. I am not dancing with her!" Rochelle cried.

"Me, neither!" Liberty said.

Miss Toni clapped her hands in the air. "Enough! Stop bickering or neither of you will dance at Leaps and Bounds. You're not dancing *together*."

"We're not?" Rochelle scratched her head. "So who is the duet with?"

The door to the studio suddenly pushed open and a tall, dark-haired teenage boy in a backward baseball cap walked in.

"With this young man," Toni said, motioning for him to come in. "Ladies, I'd like you to meet

Hayden Finley. I discovered him at the Feet on Fire competition. He lives in New Jersey, and he wants to be a guest Diva."

"Seriously? You want to be a Diva?" Rochelle asked. "You're a boy."

"And boys can't dance, right?" Hayden said. He did a smooth twirl on the floor, then stood on the tips of his jazz shoes. "How's that?"

Rochelle felt a strange flutter in the pit of her stomach—like a butterfly tickling her with its wings. "Um, okay," she said. But it was more than okay. It was amazing. Hayden could dance all right. He could dance circles around any Diva.

"But can you do lyrical? Or ballet?" Liberty challenged him.

Hayden launched into a thrilling *saut de basque*, traveling across the entire studio floor in a series of breathtaking turns. He landed on bended knee back at Liberty's feet. That shut her up. For once, Liberty was actually speechless. She couldn't take her eyes off him.

Miss Toni cleared her throat to get their

attention, but both girls were too busy staring at Hayden to hear her. "Hello?" she asked. "Can we start the choreography, or are you girls going to just stand there with your mouths hanging open?"

Hayden smiled and rose to his feet.

OMG, thought Rochelle, *he has dimples, too!*

Miss Toni continued. "Like I was saying, I envisioned a duet between a boy and a girl—and Hayden says he's up for being the male lead. That leaves the female lead."

If Rochelle was excited before, the idea of dancing with Hayden made her feel even more giddy. "So, that would be me?" she asked Miss Toni.

"Not so fast . . . ," Toni corrected her. "Liberty came to me yesterday and asked for a special dance as well. Fair is fair. She did win the National Junior Solo title."

Rochelle fumed. It was so like Liberty to try and manipulate everyone! And Miss Toni seemed to be buying it!

"So I've decided to choreograph *two* duets with Hayden. We'll try out your routines at a few of the smaller competitions. Whichever girl brings it more, gets to perform with him at Leaps and Bounds."

"So that would be me!" Liberty said, cozying up to Hayden. She batted her eyelashes. "You get to dance with the National Junior Solo champ!"

Rochelle gritted her teeth. Liberty was pulling out all the stops. First, she went behind her back to Miss Toni. Now, she was trying her best to charm Hayden into picking her as his partner.

Toni turned to Rochelle. "Your dance is called 'Inferno.' It's about a girl who is literally on fire on the dance floor," she explained. "It's a contemporary dance with Latin rhythms. A little salsa, a little *paso doble*, and lots of smoke machines."

Rochelle was confused; she had never heard of those dances before. What was Toni getting her into this time?

Hayden read her mind. "The only salsa I like is the kind you eat with tortilla chips," he joked to Rochelle. "Can I have some guacamole on the side?"

Toni ignored the wisecrack and continued. "Hayden, you will chase Rochelle around the floor, trying to capture her—but if you get too close, you get burned. Clear?"

Hayden nodded . . . then winked at Rochelle. There went that flip-flop feeling in her stomach again!

"The other duet will be between Liberty and Hayden, and I call it 'Love's First Kiss.'"

Rochelle didn't like the sound of that one bit. Especially if it meant Liberty got to lock lips with Hayden.

"It's a contemporary lyrical number set to a haunting ballad. I see you dancing in shadow behind flowing white curtains suspended from the ceiling."

"Like shadow puppets." Hayden chuckled, making a bunny with his fingers.

Toni frowned. "If we want to beat City Feet, there will be no more joking around."

The very mention of their rival dance team made Rochelle's skin crawl. City Feet Dance Studio was led by Toni's former ballet school bestie-turned-enemy Justine Chase. The Divas knew Justine had a one-track mind: all she ever thought about was one-upping Toni.

"What's with City Feet?" Hayden whispered. "Sounds like a war."

"Oh, it is," Liberty explained. "We beat them at the Reach for the Stars competition, and you can bet that evil little troll Mandy Hammond and the rest of her team are going to try everything they can to get even."

"So we kick their butts," Hayden said calmly. "Piece of cake."

Rochelle wished she had his confidence. "It's not that easy. They're good. *Really* good."

"They are." Toni overheard the conversation. "They're going to have amazing routines, perfect technique, and stunning costumes. And I have . . ."

She paused to look at Rochelle, Liberty, and Hayden. "Three students who can't focus with time ticking away."

Liberty's hand shot up. "I'm focused! I'm ready!"

"Then let's begin." Toni sighed. "We have our work cut out for us."

CHAPTER 4

Two's Company...
Three's a Crowd

Liberty had studied ballet since she was in diapers, so a *pas de deux* with Hayden was right up her alley. Rochelle watched from the corner of the studio as Hayden held her hand. Liberty rose on her toes and did a *promenade en arabesque*. It looked perfect—Liberty's leg and arm were extended elegantly behind her—but Miss Toni shook her head. "No, no. Don't think of him as a *barre*. Balance, find your stability, *then* take his hand."

Hayden smiled. "I don't mind if you lean on me now and then."

Rochelle gritted her teeth. The only thing that

made her feel a little better was Toni's relentless correcting. "Liberty! What are you doing? Why is your leg drooping and drifting? Where is your form?"

Liberty sighed. "I'm trying. I think he needs to stand closer to me."

Rochelle turned her back and tried not to watch them in the mirror. She could hear Liberty giggling.

"That's it!" Toni called. "Now look right into each other's eyes. The movement should be smooth and fluid. Liberty! Head up, shoulders back, and for goodness' sake, show me some emotion!"

"I promise not to bite," Hayden said as he inched closer. "You know, Princess Aurora does this same move with her suitors in *Sleeping Beauty*."

"Ooh!" Liberty gushed. "I would love to play Sleeping Beauty!"

"You're already a spoiled princess," Rochelle muttered under her breath.

"Enough! Enough!" Miss Toni suddenly stopped

the music. "I want to see Hayden and Rochelle now."

Rochelle sprang to attention. "I'm ready!" The silly orange ruffled skirt swirled around her hips. She felt like she was wearing a lamp shade.

"In *paso doble*, the man is the bullfighter and the woman is the cape," Miss Toni explained.

"Are you sure she's not the bull?" Liberty commented. "It suits her better . . ."

"It's all about the legs and the hips," Toni continued, ignoring Liberty. "And you need to look like a flamenco dancer, Rochelle."

She showed her how to twirl her wrists and raise them slowly over her head with a dramatic flourish. "It looks like you're clicking castanets. Get it? You do this when you split apart."

Split apart? Liberty got to spend the whole routine holding hands with Hayden, and Miss Toni was already planning how to split her and Hayden apart?

"Hayden, do this," Miss Toni commanded. She stamped her foot on the floor. "Then you take

Rochelle by the hands and turn her around—like you're twirling a cape to bait the bull."

"Bait the bull!" Liberty snickered. "This is too funny!"

"This move is called the *chasse cape*," Toni said, ignoring Liberty. "The moves of *paso doble* should all be sharp and strong."

Sharp and strong was something Rochelle could do. She darted back and forth, narrowly escaping Hayden as he chased her around the stage.

"Fierce! I want to see fire! Attack!" Miss Toni called after them.

Hayden growled at Rochelle ferociously, then laughed. "I feel like my bulldog, Buster, when he's chasing a squirrel around our backyard."

Rochelle pounced forward, practically knocking Hayden off his feet.

"That's it! That's it!" Toni shouted. "Good, Rochelle!"

"She's not *that* good," Liberty grumbled.

Hayden panted and held his hands up in surrender. "I give up! She's too fast for me."

Rochelle smiled. She loved to win—but she kind of wished Hayden had caught her.

"I'll get you next time!" Hayden vowed, trying to catch his breath.

Miss Toni looked pleased. But Liberty was brooding in the corner.

Both of these things made Rochelle happy.

"That was a good first rehearsal," Toni said. "I have lots to think about."

Rochelle hoped that one of those things was giving her the duet with Hayden. She'd never met a boy quite like him before. He was talented, cute, and funny. His only flaw, as far as she could see, was that he was nice to Liberty. Couldn't he see she was a phony? Didn't he realize she was only flirting with him so she could steal the duet and make her look bad in front of Miss Toni?

"Hayden," Liberty said, taking his arm, "let me show you around the studio. You must be starving after that workout! My housekeeper packed me a delicious snack: chocolate-covered strawberries. Care to share?"

"I love anything with chocolate," Hayden

replied. She led him through the door and into the studio hallway.

Back in the dressing room, the rest of the Divas had arrived and were warming up for their group rehearsal at noon. Rochelle couldn't hide her disappointment.

"What's wrong?" Scarlett asked. "You were so excited for your solo this morning."

"It wasn't a solo, it was a duet—which is a good thing because the guy is really cute and nice, but then Liberty was there . . . holding hands . . . and dipped in chocolate!" Rochelle blurted out.

"You're not making any sense," Bria said. "Slow down. Liberty is dipped in chocolate?"

"No, no, no." Rochelle sighed, flopping down on a bench. She explained everything: how her devious teammate had asked Miss Toni for a chance to dance with Hayden—and how she was doing everything in her power to win him over and wow their dance coach.

"Sheeshkabos!" Gracie exclaimed. "Who cares about a dumb boy?"

"Gracie has a point," Scarlett said. "Is all this fighting worth it for some guy?"

Rochelle sighed. "Hayden is not just *some* guy. He's special. He has dimples."

"My mom says there are lots of fish in the sea," Bria pointed out.

"Why are you talking about fish?" Gracie scratched her head. "Rock doesn't want a fish. She wants a boyfriend!"

"I *don't* want a boyfriend," Rochelle insisted. She turned to Scarlett. "Do I?"

Rochelle tried to get Hayden out of her head while the group entered the studio. The last thing she needed was Toni finding out she had feelings for her potential duet partner! Toni believed the only place to show emotion was on the dance floor. That's why she hardly ever cracked a smile, made a joke, or even flinched. And absolutely no one at Dance Divas had ever seen Miss Toni shed a tear—not when they lost to City Feet, not when their hot-air balloon prop once floated away midperformance, not even when Gracie kicked her in the nose doing a backflip! Toni was one tough cookie—and Rochelle had to admit, sometimes she was in awe of her. *It must be amazing to be that fierce and focused*, she thought.

"I want my strongest dancers front and center for this," Toni began, looking the girls over. "Scarlett, Liberty . . . and Rochelle."

"Me? Really?" Rochelle gasped. Usually, her coach stuck her in the back row so no one would notice her bent knees or sickled feet.

"Are you hard of hearing?" Miss Toni snapped. "I don't like to repeat myself."

Rochelle quickly moved forward next to Scarlett. She wondered what Miss Toni had in store for the group number. In the past, it had been something big, bold, and dramatic—like the "Lions, Tigers, and Bears . . . Oh, My!" number they did at the Smooth Moves competition a few months ago. They were all animals revolving around a maypole with ribbons to look like a carousel. Toni had a turntable constructed with strobe lights that barely fit in the luggage compartment under their bus. It was as "over the top" as dance competition props get. But if Rochelle knew Toni, she knew she had to have something even bigger in mind.

"You are all aware of the recent hurricane and how it impacted our state of New Jersey," she began.

Bria's hand shot up. "My school's tennis courts were totally wiped out. And my aunt Maya's basement was underwater. It was terrible."

Toni nodded. "It was. Our roof here at the studio was damaged, and we lost a few windows, but we were lucky. Some people lost their homes and even their lives. Which is why I've decided to dedicate our group number to the victims of the hurricane. Their strength and courage is going to be our inspiration."

She rolled in something that looked like a

large fountain and flicked a switch on the side. Water shot up and splashed around the center as lights turned the droplets different colors.

"Cool!" Gracie squealed. "A sprinkler!"

"Our number is called 'After the Storm,'" Toni explained. "It's about rebuilding and renewing hope and faith. There's going to be a lot of water involved. I want it to rain onstage. This little fountain is just for practice."

Liberty stuck her fingers in the stream and shuddered. "It's cold. And wet."

Rochelle splashed her. "Yeah, water usually is."

Toni nodded. "Get used to it, ladies. I want to see lots of fluid movement to match the flowing water."

Over the next three hours, Miss Toni taught them the routine. It was a powerful contemporary dance, with thunder and lightning crashing throughout the pulsing music. It was hard to keep in sync—and not slip on the wet floor—as Miss Toni barked orders.

"Put a *chaîné* in there, Bria! Gracie, keep up! You're a beat behind everyone else. And Rochelle, you're staring into space!"

Toni didn't just want the dance to be technically perfect. She wanted the audience and the judges to be moved by it. She wanted them to feel the effects and the aftermath of a hurricane. When she finally dismissed them, everyone was soggy and exhausted.

"Look on the bright side . . . we don't need to take a shower!" Scarlett said.

Rochelle wrapped a towel around her head. "Five more minutes, and she would have drowned us."

"Hey . . . did I miss the pool party?" said a voice behind them.

Rochelle spun around.

Hayden!

"Nice hairdo there, Rochelle," he joked.

She felt her cheeks flush. "Um, yeah, well, uh . . ." Rochelle knew she wanted to stay cool, calm, and sophisticated so Hayden would like her.

But her mouth and her brain just wouldn't work together! She didn't know what to say.

"Um, I, uh . . . ," she said, trying again.

"What Rock is trying to say is that we just came from group rehearsal. A big, splashy number as you can see," Scarlett piped up.

"Wow. Impressive," Hayden said. "Is this dance or synchronized swimming?"

"Can't tell you!" Scarlett said as she ushered Rochelle into the dressing room. "Big surprise!"

Rochelle rested her head in her hands. What was wrong with her? Why was she so tongue-tied around Hayden?

"You okay?" Scarlett said, putting an arm around her.

"Fine. Thanks for the save."

Scarlett smiled. "Anytime. You're right by the way . . . killer dimples."

"And Liberty is probably all over him at this very minute." Rochelle sighed.

Gracie poked her head in the dressing room. "I just met your fish," she told Rochelle. "He's really nice."

"And cool," Bria weighed in. "Did you see his sneakers? Yellow Nike LeBron X Elites? Awesome . . ."

"Great. So we're all in agreement that Hayden Finley is an amazing guy," Rochelle said. "How does this help me?"

"You're an amazing girl," Scarlett said. "So you're perfect for each other!"

If only it were that easy. If only Liberty hadn't stuck her nose in and stolen both the dance number and the guy. What had started out as a totally happy day was now the wettest, worst one ever!

CHAPTER 5

Water, Water, Everywhere

Nearly every day, Gracie changed her mind about what she wanted to be when she grew up. Some days it was an Olympic gymnast; others it was a backup dancer for Beyoncé. But this Sunday morning, it was a gourmet chef with her own restaurant.

"Breakfast is served!" she called to her mom and Scarlett. She brought a plate of waffles out of the kitchen and placed it in front of them on the dining room table.

Scarlett poked at the stack. Some of the waffles were burnt to a crisp; others were still half-frozen. "How did you cook these?" she asked.

"In the toaster." Gracie beamed. "Don't forget my secret sauce!" She pushed a plate filled with goopy red liquid in front of Scarlett.

"Honey, is that ketchup?" her mom asked, knowing Gracie's favorite ingredient.

"Not *just* ketchup," Gracie assured her, pouring a heaping spoonful over a waffle. "There's strawberries in it, too."

"Frozen strawberries," Scarlett whispered to her mom. "Help!"

"Well, Chef, you have outdone yourself; this is a meal to remember!" Her mom smiled. "Don't you think, Scarlett?"

Scarlett was trying to find an inch of waffle that was edible. "Oh, yeah. Yum."

Gracie frowned. "You're just saying you like it, Scoot," she said, calling her sister by her favorite—and Scarlett's least favorite—nickname. "You haven't eaten anything."

Scarlett poked at the gooey mess on her plate. "I don't want to eat too much before rehearsal," she said, rubbing her tummy. "It's just so delicious, I might make a pig of myself."

"Really?" Gracie asked her. "You're not fibbing?"

Scarlett tapped the tip of her nose. "Is my nose growing like Pinocchio? Then I must be telling the truth." She hoped Gracie would buy it. Just then, she heard the doorbell ring.

"Saved by the bell!" Scarlett said, jumping up from the table. "I mean, that must be Rock. Time to hit the road for the studio."

Gracie stuffed a ketchup-soaked waffle in a paper cup and skipped out the door with her dance bag.

"All aboard the Divas mobile," Rochelle's mother called from the car. Scarlett, Rochelle, and Gracie piled in the backseat and buckled up.

"Here," Gracie said, handing Rochelle the cup. "I made you breakfast-to-go."

"Thanks, Gracie," Rochelle said. "What is this?"

"Waffles à la Gracie," Scarlett said. "Go ahead . . . have a taste."

Rochelle sniffed the cup and wrinkled her nose. "Gee, I'm stuffed. Maybe later after rehearsal."

Scarlett giggled. "I'm sure Rock will work up an appetite and gobble it up."

"Cool beanbags!" Gracie exclaimed, proud of her culinary talent. "Maybe tomorrow I'll make waffles for all the Divas *and* Miss Toni."

When they arrived at the studio, Miss Toni was locked in her office.

"She's been in there for a long, long time," Bria informed them.

"We tried to eavesdrop, but the walls in here are all soundproof." Liberty sighed. "Bummer."

"What do you think it is?" Rochelle asked. She remembered the last time Toni acted secretive, the team wound up performing at the New Jersey State County Fair—dressed like ears of corn.

"Let's not panic," Scarlett said, trying to reassure them. "Maybe it's personal. Maybe she's talking to a friend."

"Does Toni have friends?" Bria asked.

"Maybe she's planning a pizza party for us,"

Gracie suggested. She still had food on the brain.

"Or maybe she's planning to kick one of us off the team," Liberty suggested. She glanced over at Rochelle. "Divas does seem to be getting a little crowded."

Just then, the lock clicked and Toni opened the door. "Is there a reason you're all standing around in the hall instead of warming up at the *barre*?" she bellowed.

Rochelle thought quickly. "We brought you breakfast! Waffles à la Gracie." She shoved the cup in Toni's face.

"How thoughtful," Toni replied. But she wasn't fooled. "I'll eat this while I watch you all do fifty push-ups." She dipped her finger in Gracie's secret sauce and took a lick. Rochelle and Scarlett gasped.

"Delish," she said, winking at Gracie. "Now hit the studio."

As they ran through their warm-up—several *pliés*, *relevés*, and *ronds de jambe* at the *barre*, Bria whispered to Rochelle. "Don't you think it's strange she hasn't told us who's getting a solo at Leaps and Bounds?"

Rochelle glanced at the calendar on the studio wall. Miss Toni had circled the date and scribbled in "Leaps and Bounds, Wilmington, Delaware" in bright red marker. The thought had crossed her mind. Since she and Liberty were locked in a battle for a duet with Hayden, that probably left Scarlett, Bria, and Gracie. Toni loved Gracie's acrobatic ability, but she knew what happened whenever she had to dance onstage alone. Gracie had terrible stage fright.

"Did she say anything to you?" Rochelle asked Scarlett.

"Nope. You?"

Scarlett shrugged. It wasn't like Toni to leave anything undecided a week before a competition—especially when they were going head to head with City Feet. She raised her hand timidly.

"Yes?" Miss Toni called on her. She was rolling the fountain into place in the center of the studio, preparing to soak them all again.

Scarlett took a deep breath. "I was just wondering if anyone will be doing a solo next weekend?"

"Absolutely," Toni replied. She went back to tinkering with the fountain.

"Are you going to tell us who?" Rochelle pressed.

"Do I have to tell you everything?" Toni replied. "Just worry about your group number. It's a hot mess. Keep stretching while I find a screwdriver."

The girls looked at one another, puzzled. What was Toni up to?

"I don't like it," Rochelle whispered. "First the secret phone call, now this?"

She turned to Liberty. "Do you know anything about this? Did you and your Hollywood hotshot mother scheme your way into a solo?"

"Puh-lease." Liberty groaned. "If I had a solo, I wouldn't keep it a secret. I'd flaunt it right in your face!"

"She has a point," Bria said.

"Then who is it?" Rochelle pondered. No one else outside of the group was prepared to be on their competition team. Unless . . .

Hayden bounded into the room. "Hey, Divas!" he said, tossing his bag and cap on the floor. He looked right at Rochelle and grinned. "What's up, Rock?"

Rochelle froze mid-*port de bras*, her hands dangling above her head.

"Snap out of it, Rock." Scarlett elbowed her. "Speak!"

"Up!" she blurted out. "I mean, nothing. Nothing's up." She quickly dropped her arms to her sides.

Liberty pushed in between them. "So, we were wondering . . . has Miss Toni talked to you about doing a solo at Leaps and Bounds next weekend?" Leave it to Liberty to get straight to the point.

"A solo? I've got my hands full learning two duets. Now she wants me to do a solo, too?" Hayden scratched his head. "Is your dance coach usually this—"

"Crazy? Definitely!" Bria piped up. "None of us were assigned a solo, so we thought it must be someone new. Like you."

Hayden shrugged. "She hasn't said anything to me."

Miss Toni returned to the studio, water hose in hand. "Hayden! Just the person I needed!"

Aha! Rochelle thought. *He is getting a solo!*

Instead, Toni handed him the hose. "Stand here and hold this tight. Be right back."

Hayden twirled the hose in his hand. "Let me guess . . . I'm supposed to be an elephant . . ." He held the hose up to his face, letting it swing in front of him. Suddenly, a blast of water sent the hose flying, whipping around the studio.

"Catch it! Catch it!" Scarlett screamed. But it was out of control, covering the walls and mirrors with a shower of water.

"I've got it!" Rochelle said, trying to tackle the hose as it flew past her. It was as slippery as a snake.

"Wait! I've got it!" Hayden called, leaping in the air.

They collided midair, landing with a *thud* on the floor, just as Miss Toni had shut off the valve.

She came into the room to see what all the commotion was about while the hose fell flat to the floor.

"Didn't I say to *hold* it?" she yelled at Hayden. He was sitting in a huge puddle on the floor next to Rochelle. Bria and Liberty had ducked behind a pile of floor mats, and Gracie and Scarlett were hiding under the piano.

"Sorry?" Hayden gulped.

"Look at this studio! It's a disaster area!" Toni fumed. "Get it cleaned up now. And you . . ." She turned to Rochelle. "Stay."

CHAPTER 6

Filling Toni's Shoes

As the Divas and Hayden hustled to get paper towels and a mop, Rochelle stood dripping wet waiting for Miss Toni to tell her off. She assumed her teacher would blame her for the hose mishap. But instead, Toni handed her a CD.

"I want you and Hayden to practice your routine as much as possible," she said.

"Really?" Rochelle could hardly believe it. Did this mean she was giving her the duet? Had she actually beaten Liberty? She had a million questions, but all she could manage to say was, "Thanks!" excitedly.

"I think you two have great chemistry," Toni continued. "But chemistry isn't enough to win. Not against City Feet."

Rochelle nodded. "Gotcha."

Just then Toni's phone rang. "Yes, this is Toni . . . ," she said before wandering off to a corner out of earshot.

Rochelle tried to make out a few words. She heard: "need a change," "flight to L.A.," and "winning team."

When she returned, Rochelle didn't let on that she had been listening in on the conversation. "I have to go out of town suddenly for a few days, and I don't want you to lose any rehearsal time," Toni told her.

"Out of town? But we just learned the choreography! How can we do this without you?"

Toni smiled ever so slightly. "Why, Rochelle. Are you saying you actually need a dance coach? I thought you preferred to do your own thing onstage rather than listen to me."

"I do. I mean, I don't. I mean, we don't know

the entire dance yet," Rochelle sputtered. How could Toni actually think of abandoning them now? The duet was all over the place and the group number—in Toni's words—was a hot mess. Even Hayden had said they needed to "smooth out the bumps." So how would they do that without Toni?

"I suppose I could get another dance instructor to step in for a few days . . ." Toni was talking to herself as she flipped through the contacts on her phone. She dialed a number, tapping her foot anxiously. "Fernando? It's Toni Moore. What are you doing this week? I need someone to come whip my dance team into shape."

Rochelle pictured a sinister lion tamer cracking a whip as the Divas cowered onstage.

"No? You're too busy. Thanks anyway."

She heard Miss Toni trying number after number, pleading with someone—anyone—to help the Divas get competition-ready.

"We can do it without a coach," Rochelle spoke up. "We know what you like and how you like it."

Toni put her phone down. "You think so, huh?" She gave Rochelle a long, hard stare. "I've never left you girls on your own before."

"We're not on our own," Rochelle insisted. "We have one another."

"Fine," Toni gave in. "I don't seem to have any other takers. But I expect it to be flawless. And since you're so sure of yourself, Rochelle, you can be in charge of the team till I return."

She grabbed her tote bag and tossed Rochelle a towel. "This studio better be dry and the group routine better be in great shape."

With that, she dashed out, ignoring the rest of the Divas as they came in to clean up.

Oh no, Rochelle thought. *What have I done? Did I just volunteer to take over for Toni?*

"Where was Toni going in such a hurry?" Bria asked. "Is she really mad at us for turning the studio into a swamp?"

Rochelle shook her soggy curls. "No, I don't think so. She got a call and then she seemed to be in a big hurry. Something about L.A. and a change of scenery."

"What?" Scarlett gasped. "She said that? What else did she say?"

Rochelle tried to remember. "All I could make out was 'winning team' and the fact that she had to leave right away."

"You don't think . . . ," Bria whispered.

"What? What?" Gracie piped up. "What don't we think?"

Liberty put her hands on her hips. "Hello? Do I need to draw a picture for you guys?" She grabbed a marker and started writing on Miss Toni's dry-erase board. "Let's review," she began, trying to sound teacherly. Rochelle rolled her eyes.

"Number one, no one has a solo and we are a week away from Leaps and Bounds." She wrote the word *solo* on the board and drew a big red X through it. "Number two, Miss Toni got a mysterious phone call." She drew a giant question mark.

"Can you get to the point?" Rochelle complained.

"And number three, she's suddenly rushing off to L.A. on a secret mission." She wrote *L.A.* with a large exclamation point next to it. "Toni is abandoning Divas for a new dance studio in L.A. That's why she hasn't bothered choreographing a solo or even finished teaching us the duets. She doesn't care."

Everyone was silently mulling over Liberty's diagram. It was a horrible thought, but it did make sense. Toni had been behaving stranger than usual lately—and she had hurried off without any explanation.

"I know Toni can do some crazy, spontaneous things sometimes, but I don't think she would just dump the Divas," Scarlett piped up. "I think she cares about all of us a lot."

Rochelle nodded. "There has to be another reason. She's gone, so let's go check out her desk and see if she left any clues."

They spent a few minutes going through Toni's drawers and notebooks. "I don't see anything in here that says 'dump the Divas,'"

Rochelle pointed out. She held up a costume sketch for the "After the Storm" number. "Why would she design costumes if she was going to leave us?"

"Let me see that," Liberty said, yanking the sketch from her hand. "There are six costumes here."

"So?" Bria asked.

"So there are only five of us. Who's the sixth girl?"

Rochelle peered closely at the drawing. There were initials under each tattered tutu that Toni had sketched: S. B., L. M., G. B., R. H., and B. C. Then there was one more: A. B.

"Maybe A. B. means 'a boy,'" Bria suggested. "Maybe it's just Hayden."

"In a tutu?" Hayden gulped, looking at the sketch. "Uh-uh. No way!"

"Maybe A. B. stands for 'Absolutely Brilliant' . . . which would be me," Liberty suggested.

Rochelle pointed to the drawing of "L. M." in a pale blue leotard with a tattered shawl around her shoulders. "Sorry. That's you, Liberty Montgomery. The one in ugly blue rags."

"There's no use trying to figure this out," said Scarlett, interrupting the bickering. "If Miss Toni wanted us to know what she was up to, she would have told us."

"So what do we do now?" Bria asked. "We have no dance coach, no costumes, and we barely have a group number."

"We just carry on and rehearse without Toni until she comes back," Rochelle told her fellow dancers. "And we have Toni's sketches, so we can ask our parents to help us make the costumes."

Liberty crossed her arms over her chest. "And who left you in charge of us?"

Rochelle took a deep breath. "As a matter of fact, Toni did. She said I'm supposed to make sure the group dance is in great shape—until she gets back."

But a single thought kept nagging at Rochelle: What if Toni didn't come back? What if the accident with the hose had actually pushed her to the breaking point? What if she had accepted a new job in L.A. coaching a new dance team, like Liberty said? Without Toni Moore, could there be any Dance Divas?

CHAPTER 7

A Team of Our Own

Rochelle stared at the compact disc Toni had given her, recalling what she had said.

"Toni must have been nuts—or desperate—to leave me in charge of our team," she told Scarlett over the phone that night.

"She trusts you. All you have to do is follow the rehearsal schedule she set up already," Scarlett replied. "You just run the rehearsal and see where we need work."

"Me? What about you?" Rochelle said. "I don't want to step on your toes. You're kind of our unofficial team leader—and you're my BFF!"

"Rock, you would not be stepping on my toes. I'd be psyched to follow your lead."

"Really?" Rochelle sighed. "Well, you're probably the only one who feels that way."

"Will you stop putting yourself down?" Scarlett insisted.

"And what about my duet with Hayden?" Rochelle added. "What if he doesn't want to be with the Divas now that Toni's not here?"

"I bet he wants to be with you," Scarlett said. "And Miss Toni did say to practice a lot . . ."

Rochelle stared up at the ceiling from her bed, hoping some answers would magically appear like diagrams on Toni's dry-erase board. She had no idea what Toni was planning or why she'd suddenly dumped all this responsibility on her shoulders.

"And don't forget the solo," Scarlett reminded her. "Someone from Divas has to do a solo at Leaps and Bounds. Miss Toni never did tell us who that would be."

Suddenly, Rochelle had an idea. "I think I

know how to decide who gets a solo fair and square."

"Without hurting anyone's feelings or making Liberty mad? How?" Scarlett asked.

"A Divas' dance-off! We let anyone on the team who wants to do a solo bring it to the dance floor. Then we invite an audience to come watch and vote. The Diva with the most votes gets to do a solo Saturday at the competition."

"That's brilliant!" Scarlett exclaimed. "And fun! Kind of like *Dancing with the Stars*, but Dancing with the Divas."

"Exactly! We let the audience choose and get in some practice before this weekend's competition."

"I know what I'm gonna do," Scarlett said. "I've always wanted to be the Sugar Plum Fairy in *The Nutcracker*."

"Go for it!" Rochelle said. "And you think you can convince Gracie to dance onstage by herself?"

"I have an idea that might work," Scarlett said.

"Awesome!" Rochelle hung up and jumped on her computer. She sent an e-mail to Bria,

Liberty, and Hayden outlining the rules of the dance-off. "Any music, style of dance, costume, or props will be permitted. The only requirements are creativity and the desire to win!"

Her in-box instantly *dinged* with a message from Bria ("Great idea!") and another from Liberty ("I am so winning that solo!"). Even Hayden responded right away: "One boy vs. five girls? Count me in!"

Then she made flyers to hang up at the studio. On a bright pink sheet of paper, she wrote:

Divas' Dance-off!
Your votes will choose a soloist for the
Leaps and Bounds competition this weekend!
Come watch the members of the
Divas elite competitive team
battle it out in the ultimate soloist showdown!
When: Wednesday at 4:00 p.m.
Where: Dance Divas Studio

"Battle it out?" Rochelle's mom said, reading over her shoulder. "Showdown? That sounds a little intense, don't you think? Are you sure Miss Toni would approve?"

"Well, she's not here, is she?" Rochelle replied. "And besides, Toni always tells us a little competition is healthy. It inspires you to be your best."

"Competition is one thing," her mom pointed out. "But this sounds like a boxing match. What's your dance?"

Rochelle thought for a moment. She'd been so preoccupied organizing the dance-off, she hadn't even considered her own routine. "I dunno," she replied. "But it has to be something really cool, really different."

"Do whatever you like, hon. As long as no weapons are involved."

"Mom, you're a genius!" Rochelle shouted, leaping up to hug her. "That's it!"

"Oh, no." Her mom hesitated. "I don't like the sound of that . . ."

"I know exactly what I'm going to do." She got a mischievous glint in her eye. "You'll just have to come to the dance-off on Wednesday to see!"

CHAPTER 8

Dancing with the Divas

Rochelle had never spent so much time in the dance studio. Usually, she was out the door as soon as Miss Toni announced, "That's a wrap for today!" But in her new position—the Divas' substitute coach—she was determined to make sure every detail of their dance-off—not to mention all the routines for Leaps and Bounds—were in order.

Liberty desperately needed a pink spotlight for her solo. "I've searched everywhere," she complained to Rochelle. "Do you know where the colored filters are?"

Rochelle hated to help Liberty, especially when

she knew all she wanted to do was beat everyone else. But she had promised Miss Toni everything would run smoothly.

"It should be in the prop closet," Rochelle told her.

"Don't you think I looked there?" Liberty said grumpily. "I couldn't find one."

Together, they went to the closet and began rummaging through piles of costumes, shoes, and assorted props, until they found a bin labeled "lighting."

"OMG, remember this?" Rochelle held up a neon green filter.

"How could I forget?" Liberty replied. "It was for our '*Wizard of Oz*-mosis' routine at regionals. I was Dorothy. You were a flying monkey. It was perfect casting."

Rochelle ignored her comment. "We all looked like aliens in that green glowing spotlight," she recalled.

"Aliens about to barf up lunch!" Liberty added, peering through the green lens.

"*Blah.*" Rochelle made a gagging noise and they

both cracked up. For a moment, they forgot to hate each other's guts.

Rochelle spotted one last box they had yet to look through. She dug deep into the bottom and pulled out a pink plastic circle. "Got it!" she said. "Found the pink filter."

Liberty grabbed it out of her hand. "Finally!" She rushed out of the prop closet, leaving Rochelle with a mess to clean up.

"Uh, you're welcome!" Rochelle called after her. Honestly, she didn't know how Toni did it! A dance coach's job was never done—and never appreciated.

Wednesday afternoon rolled around, and friends, family, and fellow dancers packed into the small auditorium at the studio. Rochelle peeked through the stage curtain. "Wow! Full house!" she exclaimed. She was wearing a white, long-sleeved turtleneck leotard, and her hair was twisted into two braided buns over her ears.

"What are you supposed to be?" Liberty smirked. "A monkey wrapped in toilet paper?"

Rochelle reached for a long wand leaning against the wall. With the flick of a switch, it glowed neon blue. "I'm dancing to the theme from Star Wars." She smiled, waving the lightsaber under Liberty's nose. "And I wouldn't mess with this Jedi warrior if I were you."

"Yeah, good luck with that," Liberty said icily. "You're going to need all the help you can get."

Rochelle noticed that she was dressed head to toe in pink—which, frankly, was not all that unusual for Liberty. But when she turned around, she saw that there was a long tail suspended from her velvet jumpsuit. Liberty secured a headband with pink velvet ears on top of her head.

"Don't tell me . . ." Rochelle groaned. "You're the Pink Panther."

"The one and only." Liberty smiled. "I'm doing a jazz and acro routine that's going to bring this audience to their feet cheering."

"Or running for the exits," Rochelle tossed back.

Scarlett stepped between them. She was dressed in a delicate pale pink tutu with a sparkling tiara on her head. "I'm sure Liberty's routine is *purr*fect," she joked. "And Rochelle, yours is stellar."

"That's so sweet of you to say, Sugar Plum Fairy," Rochelle replied. "You look great, Scarlett."

"You think?" Scarlett spun around in her toe shoes. "I have always dreamed of dancing this role."

"And I've always dreamed of dancing across a Broadway stage and seeing my name in lights on a marquee," Bria said. She had on a black tuxedo, top hat, and shiny patent leather tap shoes. She demonstrated a few quick shuffles on the hardwood floor backstage. "I'm doing a salute to Fred Astaire, one of my dance idols."

Gracie was the only one looking less than thrilled with the chance to show off onstage. "You didn't tell me there were going to be *this* many people watching!" she whispered to Scarlett. "I don't think I can do this."

"Do what? Flip some pancakes onstage?" a voice said behind her. "And here I was, thinking you were an Iron Chef."

Rochelle felt her cheeks flush. It was Hayden, and he looked heavenly. He was dressed in a dark gray suit and sporty fedora. "I'm Gene Kelly in *Singin' in the Rain*. Flooding the studio the other day gave me the idea."

"You can dance in the rain, but I'm not going out there," Gracie said, unbuttoning her white chef's coat and sitting on the floor. She crossed her legs and covered her ears so no one could talk her out of it.

"She has a little stage fright," Scarlett explained to Hayden. None of the Divas could forget the last time Gracie panicked midperformance and Scarlett had to join her onstage for an impromptu duet. To their surprise, they'd won, but Gracie still lacked the courage to compete without someone standing by her side.

"A *little* stage fright?" Liberty piped up. "She's petrified of the spotlight. I just don't get it at all."

"I do," Hayden said, sitting down on the floor next to Gracie. "I used to be terrified to go onstage in front of people when I was your age."

"You were?" Gracie asked.

"You were?" Rochelle chimed in. It seemed impossible that Hayden, with all his talent and confidence, had ever been scared of anything.

"I was, and I still am sometimes," he admitted.

"But I've tried everything. Lucky charms, deep breaths, even picturing the audience in their underwear." Gracie sighed. "It doesn't work."

"Have you tried pretending you're all alone at home, dancing in your living room?" Hayden asked. "That's what works for me when I get the jitters."

"I don't know . . ." Gracie hesitated.

"How 'bout this?" Rochelle said, handing her a pan. "Pretend you're just whipping up a Chef Gracie special."

"And don't forget this!" Scarlett said, handing

her little sister a squeeze bottle of ketchup they had brought as a prop. "Your secret ingredient."

"The more you do it, the easier it gets, Gracie," Hayden said. "I promise."

"Are you nervous now?" Gracie asked him.

Hayden winked at Rochelle. "You bet. Competing against you Divas is pretty scary. I'm afraid you're gonna kick my butt."

"You're forgetting one thing," Rochelle said, crouching down next to him. For once, she wasn't afraid to speak or look him in the eyes. Taking over and leading the team these past few days had given her newfound confidence. "You're a Dance Diva, too."

"I'm honored," Hayden replied. "But could I maybe be a Dance Divo . . . or Dude . . . something that sounds a little tougher?"

Rochelle tapped the lightsaber sitting in a holster on her hip. "Are you saying Divas aren't tough?"

Gracie stood up. "Hey, don't pick on my boyfriend, Rock!" She put on her chef's hat and stood up. Then she planted a kiss on Hayden's forehead.

"OMG! Your little sis just stole Rock's guy," Bria whispered to Scarlett.

This time, it was Hayden's turn to blush. "You go out there, Gracie, and show 'em how it's done. I'll *ketchup* with you later. Get it?"

Gracie cracked up and grabbed her ketchup bottle.

"Kaydokey," Gracie replied.

Scarlett smiled. That was Gracie's way of saying okay and okeydokey rolled into one. Hayden had really gotten through to her! Rochelle had put her third in the lineup, but now she wanted to go on first.

"Your BF is amazing," Scarlett whispered to Rochelle.

"He's not my BF." Rochelle sighed. "He's my dance partner."

" 'You say potato, I say *potahto* . . . ,' " Bria sang, just like Fred Astaire. "If he's not your boyfriend, I'll eat my top hat."

Rochelle glanced back at Hayden. He did look a little nervous as he stretched and warmed up for his solo. Maybe he was telling the truth. Maybe he wasn't as confident as he pretended to be. Maybe he felt the same butterflies in his stomach that she felt as they darted around the dance floor. Could it be that all along Hayden liked her, too?

"You have a packed theater—don't you think it's time to start the show?" A stern yet familiar voice snapped Rochelle back to her senses.

"I can't wait to see what you girls have done while I was gone," Miss Toni said. She glared at Rochelle. "Especially you."

CHAPTER 9

Showdown!

Rochelle walked onstage with a microphone in hand, ready to announce the start of the dance-off. She felt her knees shaking. The last thing she expected was for Miss Toni to return today!

"Ladies and gentlemen, thank you all for coming," she said nervously. "We hope you like our show and vote for your favorite solo at the end. You'll find ballots on your chairs. Please fill them out and put them in the boxes at the back of the auditorium after the show."

She scanned the audience for Miss Toni's face. Where was that tight black bun and bright red lipstick? And was Toni going to kill her as soon as the show was over? Then she spied another familiar face in the front row and gasped. It was one of the dancers from City Feet, Anya Bazarov. Anya had caused quite a scandal at Feet on Fire. She was an amazing ballerina, but Justine had registered her to compete as a Junior Soloist when she was thirteen and actually no longer a Junior. It had gotten her disqualified for her solo, and points had been deducted from City Feet's group score. It was part of the reason Dance Divas won that competition.

Rochelle panicked: Was Anya out for revenge? Was she there to spy on them and report back to Justine? She raced back to the wings. "Guys, you won't believe who's out there! That Bizarre-o girl from City Feet!"

"No way!" Scarlett said. "What's she doing here?" She peeked out of the curtain to get a closer look.

"Rock," Bria said solemnly. "There's something else you should see."

There, seated right next to Anya, was Miss Toni.

"Wait a sec. Weren't the initials on Toni's costume sketch 'A. B.'?" Bria recalled.

"And doesn't Anya come from L.A.?" Liberty pointed out.

"No way!" Rochelle cried. "Miss Toni stole Anya away from City Feet to be a Diva!"

"That would be really sneaky," Bria said.

"That would be really smart," Liberty added. "Without Anya, City Feet doesn't stand a chance of beating us."

Rochelle refused to believe Toni could play dirty like this. Yes, she wanted to win against City Feet, but she would never purposely do something to destroy another team's chances. Would she?

"*Ahem.*" Gracie cleared her throat. "I think it's my turn. Rock, introduce me!" She smiled at Hayden adoringly. "Watch this!"

Rochelle returned to the stage, trying not to look at her teacher or Anya. Instead, she smiled and put on her best emcee voice: "Please welcome to the stage, Gracie doing an acro routine to 'Cooking by the Book'!"

Gracie skipped out onstage and stood before the toy kitchen set that Scarlett had prepared for her. There was a bunch of pots and pans, spoons and mixing bowls—and of course, pancakes and ketchup. Her song was a fun, upbeat tune, and the audience clapped along as she flipped a pancake in a frying pan, then did a perfect back handspring step out. She ended the routine with a side aerial and a chin stand.

"That little Gracie's got moves," Hayden said from the wings.

"You really helped her conquer her fear today," Scarlett said. "You made her feel like she could do anything. Thanks."

"Yeah, I have that effect on people. Right, Rock?" Hayden teased.

Rochelle smiled. "You're up next, Dance Divo. Let's see what you got."

As Gracie took her bows, Hayden rolled the kitchen set offstage and pushed out his prop: an old-fashioned streetlamp he'd borrowed from his school theater department.

"Doing a contemporary routine to 'Singin' in the Rain,' please give it up for Hayden!" Rochelle announced.

As the music began, Hayden opened his black umbrella and stretched his hand toward the sky. He leaped up on the lamppost and tossed his hat and umbrella to the side of the stage. He swung around the post and dismounted, rolling into a front somersault. Then he danced around the stage and performed a breathtaking *cabriole*—a scissorlike leap in the air that made the audience applaud wildly.

"Whoa!" Scarlett exclaimed. "He's incredible."

"He is, isn't he?" Liberty swooned.

"He's mine. Hands off!" Gracie said, giving Liberty a little shove.

As he took his bows, Hayden scooped up his hat and placed it back on his head. He looked to the wings and tipped it at Rochelle. Her heart did a little tap dance.

"Rock, you're next," Scarlett said. "I'll introduce you."

Scarlett walked across the stage as the lights dimmed. "Performing a contemporary routine to the Star Wars theme, please welcome our Divas director for this dance-off, Rochelle!"

Rochelle smiled. "Divas director" had a nice ring to it. These past few days, she'd really given it her all, never once complaining, even when Liberty tried to rattle her. She helped each of her team members with their music, costumes, and props. She handed out flyers and printed up programs and ballots so the audience could vote. It was an exhausting amount of work to do, and it made her appreciate Miss Toni a little more. Coaching a dance team was not an easy job!

As the orchestral theme from Star Wars boomed over the speakers, Rochelle exploded onstage, swinging her lightsaber through the air. She felt like Princess Leia, leading the Rebel Alliance into battle against the Death Star. Her *grand jeté* was sharp and clean—a perfect split midair. And as she did an *échappé sauté*, she seemed magically suspended above the ground for a few seconds.

When the number ended, she saw that the audience was cheering and giving her a standing ovation. Even Toni was on her feet, applauding.

From the wings, she heard her fellow Divas calling, "Brava!" Hayden was the first to greet her.

"Awesome! You rocked it, Rock," he said enthusiastically. Then he grabbed her in a big bear hug.

Rochelle was stunned. "Thanks," she said breathlessly. He was still hugging her, and she hoped he'd never let go.

"No fair! You like her more than me!" Gracie pouted. Rochelle suspected Liberty was thinking the same thing.

"You haven't seen my routine yet, Hayden," Liberty said, practically pulling him away from Rochelle. "I'm next. You've never seen anything like this."

She strutted out onstage, microphone in hand, to introduce herself to the crowd. "Hi, everyone! I'm Liberty and I'm going to be doing a jazz routine choreographed by my famous mother, Jane Montgomery. It's called 'Pink Panther Revisited.'"

"I thought her mom was in L.A.," Rochelle whispered to Bria.

"Choreo-Skype." Bria sighed. "She even Fed-Exed the costume so Liberty would have nothing but the best. Britney Spears's costume designer made it for her."

"She's really something, isn't she?" Hayden said, then whistled through his teeth. Rochelle couldn't tell if that was a compliment or a criticism. But he seemed riveted as Liberty slunk around the stage and purred like a kitty. Even she had to admit that her teammate's moves were exquisite. How did Liberty get her leg up so high and not lose her balance?

At the end of the routine, she zipped off the catsuit to reveal a pink sequin leotard beneath it. She did an amazing thirty-one *fouetté pirouettes* as the crowd clapped and counted.

"That is sick!" Hayden gushed. "Liberty deserves to win."

Rochelle's heart sunk. Hayden thought Liberty was the best dancer—and as much as it pained her to admit it, he was right. Not even Scarlett's graceful Sugar Plum or Bria's exciting tap routine that followed could top Liberty's nonstop spins. No matter how hard Rochelle tried, Liberty would always be better than she was.

CHAPTER 10

The Envelope, Please

"Everyone is done voting," Scarlett told Rochelle during the intermission. "Your mom said she'll tally the votes and we can announce the winner after the break."

"Why bother counting the votes?" Rochelle sighed. She saw that Liberty was chatting with Hayden in a corner. She was giggling and demonstrating her *pirouettes* for him. "We already know who won."

"You do?" Gracie asked. "I wanna know, too!"

Scarlett shook her head. "Rock doesn't know who won. She's just feeling defeated."

Gracie looked puzzled. "Da feeted? What's wrong with da feet?" she asked Rochelle, staring at her toes. "Are they hurting you? Maybe you should stretch?"

Rochelle laughed and gave Gracie a hug. "What would I do without you, Gracie?"

"You'd have a ketchup-less life, that's for sure," Scarlett said, and chuckled.

The Divas waited anxiously as Rochelle's mom tallied the votes. She double-checked everything before writing a name down on a slip of paper.

"Who got the solo?" Gracie asked, bouncing up and down. "I hope it was me!"

"You were all absolutely brilliant," Mrs. Hayes said. "But I am sworn to secrecy." She handed a sealed envelope to Rochelle. "Go ahead, honey. Read the results onstage before Gracie turns into a human pogo stick!"

Rochelle stepped nervously out into the spot-light once again. She adjusted the microphone stand and summoned everyone to attention. "Excuse me! Can we have everyone take their seats? We have the winner of the dance-off."

She gently tore open the envelope and pulled out the folded slip of paper inside. "And the winner of the solo at Leaps and Bounds is . . ." She opened the paper and saw the name. It couldn't be!

"Hayden Finley."

Hayden bounded onto the stage, pumping his fist in the air. "Yes! I won!" he exclaimed as the audience applauded wildly.

"Encore! Encore!" they called.

"Well, you should give them what they want," Rochelle said.

"Only if we do our duet," Hayden replied. "Come on. Let's give them a sneak peek. We have the smoke machine backstage."

Rochelle panicked. "Wait! I can't! We're not ready! We don't have our music."

Scarlett handed her the CD Toni had given Rochelle for practice. "You're as ready as you'll ever be. Go ahead, Rock. Show 'em what you got."

"But I don't have my skirt," Rochelle said nervously.

"Here, improvise," Bria said, tying a ballet wrap sweater around her waist.

"But, but . . . ," Rochelle said, trying to think of another excuse, just one more reason why she couldn't go out onstage and dance with Hayden.

He held his hand out to her. "You coming?" He smiled and Rochelle's hesitation melted away.

As their music started, Rochelle dashed out onto the stage, lunging at Hayden as he did his best to catch her in his arms. A white smoke billowed out of the machine, making it hard to see. Rochelle could barely find Hayden in all that fog, but she trusted he would be there beside her. Every time he moved forward, she stepped back; it was thrilling choreography that had the audience on the edge of their seats.

As she broke away into her *piqué* turns, she heard her fellow Divas cheering from the wings.

She remembered everything Toni taught her. She pointed her right leg straight out into the floor and came up into a *passé* with her left. Then she spun, trying to keep her eyes focused on a spot on the back wall of the theater. But the smoke was stinging her eyes. She was concentrating so hard as she traveled across the stage that she didn't notice the sweater coming loose around her hips. It fell to the floor, and she didn't see it beneath her feet. She tripped and fell, landing on the stage with a hard *thud*.

"Oh, no!" Scarlett yelled. "Stop the music!" As Bria raced for the sound system, Scarlett ran out to her best friend.

"Are you okay, Rock?" she asked, worried. She knew how embarrassing it was to fall during a routine. She'd done it herself in competition.

"It hurts really bad," Rochelle said, holding her ankle.

In seconds, Toni was up on the stage beside her, along with Rochelle's mom.

Toni kneeled down to examine her. "It looks

swollen. Can you put any pressure on it?" Rochelle tried to stand and winced in pain.

"I'm so sorry, Rock," Hayden said. "It was my dumb idea to have you do our duet." His blue eyes looked worried and sincere.

"I'm the one who told you to tie the sweater around your waist," Bria said. "I'm sorry!"

"I think we should get you to the emergency room to make sure it's not broken," Toni said. She too looked concerned.

"A hospital?" Rochelle gulped. She'd never been in a hospital, and the thought of all those lights and machines and doctors terrified her.

"Don't worry, honey. It'll be okay," her mom said, holding her hand.

Rochelle limped out of the studio, leaning on Hayden. It made her feel a tiny bit better to have his arms around her. But right now, all she could think about was one thing: What if her ankle was broken? What if she could never dance again?

CHAPTER 11

The Show Must Go On

After waiting for hours in the emergency room of the Scotch Plains Medical Center, Rochelle was finally taken in for X-rays.

The doctor studied her chart and examined her ankle. "Does this hurt?" he asked.

"Ouch! Yes!" Rochelle answered, her eyes brimming with tears.

"Well, the good news is, there's no break. The bad news is, you have a bad sprain and you have to be off your feet and on crutches."

"For how long?" Rochelle asked.

"A little while," the doctor replied. "Four weeks."

Four weeks! That meant no competing in Leaps and Bounds this weekend! That meant no duet with Hayden! That meant no Divas for a month!

"But the competition!" she moaned. "My team!"

"Honey, you'll be fine," her mother said, trying to comfort her. "The doctor said you'll be good as new in four weeks."

"If you stay off that foot," Miss Toni interjected. "And I am not risking you injuring it worse by not listening to the doctor's orders."

"I'm going to tape it up and splint it, and show you how to use the crutches," the doctor continued. "I'm afraid you'll be in a boot for a while—not your pretty dance shoes."

Rochelle couldn't believe what she was hearing. She felt like her whole world was crumbling around her. She had never deserted the Divas before. They needed her! "What about the group routine? What about City Feet?"

"Don't worry about that. I always have a Plan B," Toni told her. She patted her on the shoulder. "What's important is that you're okay."

As Rochelle hobbled out of the hospital room on her crutches, all her teammates were gathered in the waiting room. They had balloons, teddy bears, and Gracie was holding a giant Hershey's Kiss.

"Rock!" Scarlett cried, running to hug her. "We were so worried about you! Are you okay?"

"Yeah," Rochelle said. "Just out of commission for a month."

"What?" Bria gasped. "You can't dance?"

"No, both the doctor and Toni gave me strict orders to stay off my ankle."

She glanced over at Liberty. "Go ahead. Celebrate. You won the duet with Hayden this weekend after all."

She expected Liberty to smirk or rub it in her face. But instead she said, "I didn't want to win in that way. It's no fun if I can't kick your butt."

"We all want you to be back on your feet," Hayden said, coming forward with a bouquet of red roses. "Especially me."

Rochelle blushed, but not even Hayden's sweet sentiment could cheer her up. All she wanted was to go home and curl up in a ball on her bed and cry.

The next day at the Divas studio only made Rochelle feel worse. All the girls were dressed and ready to run the group number while she hobbled in and sat in a chair in the corner.

When Toni walked in the studio, she had a guest with her: Anya.

"Divas, Hayden, I think you all know Anya Bazarov, formerly of City Feet?"

"Formerly?" Liberty asked. "As in, she's not on their team anymore?"

"Precisely," Toni replied.

"So whose team *is* she on?" Scarlett asked cautiously.

Toni gave Anya a gentle push into the center of the studio floor. "I think I'll let her tell you."

The girl took a deep breath and started to explain. "What Justine did . . . telling everyone I wasn't thirteen yet just so I could beat you guys in the Junior division . . . that was cheating."

Liberty nodded. "Yeah. No kidding."

"Well, my parents and I decided I shouldn't be on a team with people who do that. So I quit City Feet, and we called Miss Toni."

"You called her?" Rochelle asked. "She didn't steal you away from City Feet?"

Toni frowned. "Do you girls honestly believe I would do that? I'm only trying to help Anya since she has no dance team and wants to stay in New York City. I went all the way to L.A. to talk to her and her parents and they begged me to take her. Frankly, we'd be lucky to have her—especially with Rochelle off her feet."

"So she's going to be in the group number Saturday?" Scarlett asked.

"Well, since you went through the costume sketches on my desk, you already know that," Toni said, turning to retrieve the fountain from the back of the studio.

"How did you know we looked in your desk?" Gracie gasped.

Toni pointed to the bun on the back of her head. "I have eyes in here."

"Whoa. That is greepy!" Gracie said.

"Translation: gross and creepy," Scarlett whispered to her teammates.

"And I also have robot ears that hear for miles around," Toni called. A hush fell over the studio. "Which is greepier."

"So I will teach Anya the choreography, and she will fill in for Rochelle," their teacher continued. "Where are we with the costumes?"

Rochelle pulled a yellow skirt out of her dance bag. The fabric was torn into shreds. "Our moms helped us make these," she said.

"They're not bad," Toni said, fingering the fringe. "But they're too pretty. They need to look like you've been in a hurricane. I need dirty, torn, tattered." She took the skirt out of Rochelle's hand and threw it on the floor. "Gracie," she said. "Come jump up and down on this."

The little girl happily obeyed until the fabric was covered with dark smudges from her worn ballet slippers and wrinkles. "I want each of you to take your skirts home and do the same. Maybe even run them over with your bikes a couple of times."

"This is the funnest homework ever," Gracie said, giggling.

Rochelle sighed. She wouldn't be biking or jumping up and down for four weeks. She'd even miss getting soaking wet in rehearsals.

Toni turned to Liberty. "When I was in L.A., I spoke to your mother about the rain we need for our number. She generously offered to have one of her FX crew help out. We're going to have a rain curtain that falls behind you guys—so you won't be slipping everywhere and getting soaked."

Liberty beamed. Since her mother was providing the props, that meant Toni owed her a favor.

"And if Rochelle can't do her duet with Hayden this weekend, I can do mine, right?" she asked Toni.

"Yes, you can do 'Love's First Kiss' with Hayden, and he gets the solo—per your dance-off rules," Toni replied. "But I am putting in two more solos that will knock the judges' socks off. Anya will do one, and Gracie, you'll do the other. Your cooking routine was hot stuff."

Before Gracie could even hesitate, Hayden patted her on the back. "Go, Gracie!" He winked. "You and me soloing!" Gracie smiled.

So that was it, Rochelle thought. *Everyone was getting what they wanted—except for her.*

Toni must have read her mind. "And since Rochelle was such a great Divas director in my absence, I am going to make her my official assistant for Leaps and Bounds—if she thinks she can handle it."

Rochelle smiled. No Diva had ever "assisted" Toni. Usually one of the dance instructors or choreographers tagged along to direct the activity from the wings. It felt awesome that Toni trusted her so much—especially when she saw Liberty squirm. "Yes! I can do it!"

"It means making sure all your teammates are set backstage at the competition; that all the music, scenery, and props are ready; that everything down to the last tiny detail is accounted for. I'll be in the audience watching, and I won't tolerate any mistakes."

Rochelle looked over at Scarlett, who was giving her two thumbs-up. "I can handle it," she said firmly.

Toni strolled over to the calendar on the wall and pointed to the red circle on Saturday. "We only have two days to fix these dances," she said sternly. "I want to see sweat, and I want to see perfection." Every head in the studio nodded. "Next stop: Leaps and Bounds."

CHAPTER 12

Sticks and Stones

As the Dance Divas' bus pulled up to the entrance of a small school, Toni stuck her head out the window. There was a banner out front that read, "GO, BULLDOGS!"

"This is it?" she asked. "This is Leaps and Bounds. Are you sure?"

The bus driver nodded. "This is the place."

Rochelle hoped the GPS knew what it was doing. They'd competed in huge hotels, mammoth convention centers, even theme parks. But never before in a school.

"This should be interesting." Their dance

coach sighed. "Remember, girls . . . and boy . . . no fraternizing with the enemy."

"What does that mean?" Gracie asked, tugging on Miss Toni's coat.

"It means if you see Justine, or Mandy or any of the other City Feet dancers, don't talk to them."

Toni strode up the steps of the high school to the entrance and pushed through the big red doors. The Divas followed, heads held high, while Rochelle hobbled behind. Inside, there were already numerous dance troupes checking in at registration.

"Where's the stage?" Toni asked. "And the dressing rooms?"

A boy behind the desk motioned to the right. "There is no stage. The dance competition is in the gymnasium. And the locker rooms are that-away."

"Seriously? Is this a dance competition or gym class?" Liberty complained.

"We'll make the best of it," Toni said, grabbing their credentials and checking the lineup.

"Sorry . . . if we knew you were coming, we would have rolled out the red carpet," said a voice behind them.

Toni didn't even have to turn around. "Justine," she said, smiling through gritted teeth. "Did you just arrive here on your broomstick?"

"Wow," Hayden whispered to Rochelle. "You weren't kidding about things getting ugly between Divas and City Feet."

"It hasn't even started." Scarlett sighed, watching Mandy and the rest of her team stroll through the doors of the high school. "Here comes trouble."

"If she opens her mouth, I swear I'm gonna trip her with my crutches," Rochelle said bristly.

Mandy, the seven-year-old "Tiny Terror" of City Feet, made a beeline right for Gracie. It was much easier to pick on someone her own size. "Miss Justine says you're a scaredy-cat—and that my aerials are way higher than yours."

Scarlett was about to defend her sister, but Liberty stopped her.

"I got this," she said, ignoring Miss Toni's order not to talk to City Feet. "If it isn't Mandy Mouse." Liberty grinned. "So nice to see you and your Stinky Feet again. Would you like to congratulate us now or later for beating you today? Your choice."

"Ouch!" Hayden commented. "That's gotta hurt."

"Sometimes I really love Liberty," Scarlett remarked. "She always knows just what to say."

"I'm glad she's on our team . . . and not theirs," Bria added.

"Our coach told us not to listen to you," Mandy said with a sniff. "You're just little mosquitoes, buzzing in our ears. *BUZZ, BUZZ, BUZZ.*"

"And you know what happens to mosquitoes," said Regan, another girl on the City Feet team. She was eleven, the same age as Scarlett, Rochelle, Liberty, and Bria, and she wore her dark hair in a short pixie cut. Rumor had it that Justine was grooming her for stardom. She clapped her hands together. "SWAT!"

Anya suddenly stepped forward. "I wouldn't be too sure about that," she said.

Regan froze; she and Anya had been friends on City Feet. "You're on their team? I thought you went back home to L.A."

"Well, of course she is," Liberty quipped. "She wants to be on the winning team . . . not with the losers."

"Well, we don't need Anya," Mandy shot back. "We have Addison." A tall, blond teenage girl stepped forward. She was wearing the City Feet black-and-white satin jacket.

"Hey," she said simply.

"Hay is for horses, Baddison—didn't Miss Justine teach you that?" Liberty chuckled.

"No, but she did teach me to do fifty *fouettés* in a row—which is more than you can do," Addison replied, grinning. "Unless you'd like to prove me wrong."

"Anytime," Liberty growled back.

"Ladies, ladies," Hayden said, pulling Liberty away from their rivals. "Can't we all just be friends?"

"Who's this? Your bodyguard?" Addison taunted them.

"Ha-ha! The Divas are scared of us! They need a bodyguard to protect them!" Mandy said, laughing.

"You just bring it!" Rochelle exclaimed. "I am so gonna kick your butt, you mean little munchkin!" Then she remembered she was in a cast and on crutches. The entire City Feet team erupted in laughter.

"OMG, that is too funny!" Regan laughed. "Look, Rochelle has a boo-boo! I wonder how many *pirouettes* you can do in that thing!" She snapped a photo of the ugly black boot on Rochelle's foot. "I'm so posting this on Instagram!"

Justine grabbed the iPhone out of her hand. "You'll do nothing of the kind," she commanded. "We do our fighting on the dance floor." With that, she ushered her team down the hall.

Hayden shook his head. "I take back everything I ever said about Divas not being tough."

"Are you proud of yourselves?" Toni asked. She

had seen the whole argument go down. "Didn't I tell you to steer clear of City Feet?"

"Mandy started it," Gracie tattled. "She called me a scaredy-cat."

"I don't care what she said or what any of them said. We don't stoop to their level."

Gracie raised her hand. "Miss Toni, does Justine really have a broomstick like you said? Is it like the one in *Harry Potter*?"

Rochelle giggled. Leave it to Gracie to call Toni out!

"No, I was making a joke. But you're right—it wasn't funny and it wasn't nice. So let's all just forget about City Feet and focus on our own team."

In the gymnasium, Scarlett felt the floor with her jazz shoe. It was rock hard and slippery with wax.

"We're not used to dancing on a floor like this," she told Toni.

"A dancer can dance anywhere," Toni replied. "Fred Astaire danced on the ceiling." She climbed up on a ladder to check that the PVC pipe Liberty's mom had sent them was properly hung from the gym ceiling and rigged to a water hose.

"Is that our hurricane?" Anya asked.

"Hopefully," Toni said. "The holes should let the water from the hose trickle through behind you. And the trough on the floor should catch it and keep the floor dry. It'll look like a curtain of rain behind you."

Toni continued talking—more to herself than to any of the Divas. "We need to make sure the thunder and lightning goes off on time . . . and the wind machine is blowing hard enough so the judges can feel it in their faces. Rochelle? Are you paying attention?"

Rochelle was sitting on the bleachers, watching Liberty and Hayden run their routine in the corner of the gym. She knew it was just acting, but they did look like a couple in love, especially when Hayden lifted her high overhead, then gently cradled her in his arms. Watching them only made her feel worse, but she couldn't look away.

"Did you hear anything I just said?" Toni asked.

Rochelle jumped to attention. "Sorry. What?"

Toni sighed and sat down next to her.

"Marcus Sanzobar," her teacher said quietly.

"Huh?"

"Marcus Sanzobar was the boy my teacher Miss Olga paired me with in *pas de deux* class at ABC."

Rochelle sensed a tale about Toni's teen years at American Ballet Company coming on. Her teacher was very tight-lipped about her past, and only shared details when she had an important point to make—a moral to her story. So Rochelle listened carefully.

"Marcus was an amazing dancer," Toni said. "I loved to watch him. He was so dynamic as Franz in *Coppélia*."

"Was he cute?" Rochelle asked.

"The cutest," Toni replied. "He had blond hair and green eyes that twinkled in the spotlight. We hung out together after ballet class every day. We'd eat pizza, play video games. Then one day, he called me Swanilda."

"Ugh!" Rochelle made a face. "That's an awful thing to call anyone!"

"No! No!" Toni corrected her. "It's a lovely thing to call your girlfriend. Swanilda is the girl who wins Franz's heart in *Coppélia*."

"So, he was your BF?"

Toni smiled. "My first BF ever. Justine got to dance with him quite a bit at ABC as she made her way up the ranks there."

"Oh, no! Justine stole your boyfriend?" Rochelle cried. "That's terrible!"

"No, that's the point. She didn't. She tried her hardest, but Marcus was never interested in her, only her dancing. You see what I'm saying?"

Rochelle slowly nodded her head. "That I shouldn't worry about Liberty doing a duet with Hayden?"

"Exactly!" Toni said, patting her on the arm. "What you should worry about is the wind machine, Swanilda."

Rochelle checked and double-checked that all the Divas' music was ready, and all their props were in place and working. "Don't forget, Anya," she reminded her new teammate. "You enter down the ramp."

She pointed to a white wooden wedge Toni had stowed in the wings. Anya was dancing the role of Nikiya, a royal temple dancer, from the ballet *La Bayadère*. It was Toni's idea to dress her in a flowing white handkerchief skirt, a silver beaded halter top, and a white chiffon veil draped over her face. The dance called for incredible grace and beautiful long lines—both were Anya's specialty. But Anya wasn't too sure about the veil.

"It's kind of hard to see through," she told Rochelle. "I'm afraid I'm going to fall down the ramp. Or worse, into the judges' laps! Then there's this . . ."

She held up a porcelain water jug Miss Toni had brought along on the bus. "She wants me to balance it on my head. Seriously! It weighs a ton!"

Rochelle laughed. "Okay, that's pretty funny. Toni does have a talent for throwing things into the routines at the very last minute."

Anya placed the jug on her head and tried to

steady it. Every time she took her hands away, it wobbled, threatening to crash to the floor. "This is hopeless!" she cried.

"If you want my advice . . . ," Rochelle began.

"Yes! Please!" Anya pleaded. "I don't want to make a complete fool out of myself in front of City Feet—not to mention the entire audience!"

Rochelle knew Toni hated when anyone changed her choreography, but she had appointed her assistant dance coach, hadn't she? "Lose the veil over your face and drape it down your back instead, so it flies out behind you as you do your *tour jetés*. And carry the jug on your shoulder . . . but just for your entrance. When you're done with your dance, you can pick it up again and bow to the audience—like you're a servant, bowing before the Indian Royal Court. It'll be very dramatic."

"Thank you!" Anya said, hugging her. "That's so much better."

Gracie also had an issue with her solo. Miss Toni had rigged the pancakes on the stove to flip up in the air just as she did her backflip.

"It's stuck," Gracie said. "I keep hitting the button, but they just keep sitting there."

"I'll take care of it," Rochelle assured her. "It's probably a short circuit in the trigger."

Last but not least, Hayden had a problem with his umbrella. "Toni wants it to fly out of my hand on an invisible wire," he said, demonstrating. The umbrella was supposed to float above his head while he did his routine. Instead, it levitated a few inches off the ground and stayed there.

"I think it just needs a little boost. The umbrella's probably too heavy. I'll look into it," Rochelle promised.

By the five-minutes-to-curtain call, she thought she had fixed all the Divas' dilemmas. She was sure Miss Toni would be proud of her handling everything so calmly and efficiently. *Who knows,* Rochelle pondered, *maybe she'll even make me her permanent assistant.*

The announcer welcomed the crowd and announced the first competitor in the Petite Solo category. "Please give a round of applause for

Mandy doing an acro routine to 'Red, Red Robin'!"

Mandy burst onto the gym floor in a series of tumbles, twists, and flips. She flapped her arms and wiggled the red feathers sewn to the backside of her costume. She chirped, whistled, and made cute, pouty faces at the judges.

"Ugh, this dance is for the birds!" Liberty groaned, watching from the sidelines. "Gracie, your routine is so much better than this! Gracie?"

Everyone suddenly realized Gracie was nowhere to be found. "Maybe she went to the bathroom?" Scarlett suggested. "I'll go check!"

"I'll check the locker room," Bria said.

"Liberty and I will check the vending machines," said Anya. "Maybe she got hungry and went for a snack."

Rochelle looked at the lineup listed in the program. "She's the third dancer up in Petite Solo—we don't have a lot of time! Find her! Fast!"

"I have a hunch where she may be," Hayden said. "Give me a sec."

"Where?" Rochelle asked. She was frantic. If Gracie missed her cue, Toni would punish them all, starting with her assistant.

Hayden walked outside the gym and found what he was looking for: the broom closet. He slowly opened the door and peered inside. There, seated on the floor among the mops and buckets, was Gracie.

"Hey, you," Hayden said gently. "You found my special hiding place."

"Your hiding place? This is my hiding place," she insisted.

"Nuh-uh," Hayden insisted. "I've been hiding in broom closets for about seven years. Nobody ever thinks to look in here, you know."

"Except you," Gracie pointed out. "Are you gonna make me go back out there?"

Hayden shook his head. "Nope. Not if you don't want to go beat Mandy. I totally understand."

Gracie bit her nails. "Well, I wanna beat Mandy. But I'm not sure I can."

"I'm sure you can't beat her sitting in here,"

Hayden said. "There's nothing to be scared of, you know. There's not even a stage—just a gym floor. And you're used to tumbling on those all the time, right?"

Gracie mulled it over. "It's not a stage, is it?"

"Nope, just a big ol' gym with bleachers. No sweat. I'm not even nervous about going up against City Feet."

"You're not? How come?" Gracie asked.

"Because feet always stink," he joked, waving his toes in her face. "Am I right or am I right?"

"*Eww!*" Gracie said, giggling and holding her nose.

He stood up and offered Gracie his hand. "You coming? I'm kind of starving. So when you're done with your dance, can you save me a pancake—with ketchup, please?"

"Next up in the Petite Solo division, we have Gracie doing an acro routine to 'Cooking by the Book'!" Rochelle's heart was pounding as the announcer called Gracie's name. She saw Toni's face in the audience. She looked livid.

"Do we have Gracie? Is she in the gym?" the announcer said, trying again. "Last call for Gracie . . ."

"Here!" said a small voice. Gracie appeared at the door of the gym holding Hayden's hand. Rochelle was relieved to see she didn't look scared at all. She was smiling and waving at the audience.

"Quick! Get into your costume!" Rochelle said, tying Gracie's apron over her red leotard and securing her chef's hat with a few bobby pins. The littlest Diva took her place onstage just as the music started to play.

She saw Toni making her way over from the bleachers.

"What happened?" she demanded. "Divas don't miss their cues."

"No biggie," Hayden said, trying to assure her. "Gracie just got a little lost in the hallway."

She gave Rochelle her iciest look. "It's your job

to make sure everything goes according to plan. You wanted to be my assistant."

"I know . . . I'm trying!" Rochelle said. "There are just so many little details."

"Welcome to my world," Toni said. "If you can't take the heat, then get out of the kitchen."

CHAPTER 13

Hayden the Hero

Rochelle crossed her fingers that Gracie would get through her routine without any further drama. Each of her flips was flawless, and the judges smiled as she did a spider walk around the gym floor. Finally, it was time for the big finale: her backflip timed to the pancake flip. She hit the button on the stove and the pancakes catapulted into the air. Thank goodness! Rochelle breathed a sigh of relief. Then she watched in horror as one climbed higher and higher till it landed—*KER-SPLAT!*—right on the bald head of one of the judges! The entire gym roared with laughter.

Gracie looked startled; Rochelle prayed she

wouldn't burst into tears. Instead, she cracked up as well. Luckily, the judge was a good sport. He pulled the pancake off his head and took a bite.

"That was a delicious routine," the announcer joked as Gracie skipped back to the sidelines.

"I did it! I did it!" she squealed.

"You sure did!" Scarlett said, hugging her little sister. "I'm so proud of you, Gracie!"

"Me, too." Hayden smiled, high-fiving her. "Nice job. You showed that Mandy who's boss."

Rochelle saw Mandy standing with her team on the opposite side of the gym. She didn't look happy. *One down*, she thought, *a few more to go.*

Junior Solos were up next. City Feet's Regan did a bold Broadway-style dance number from *Anything Goes*, dressed in a sailor hat and blue sparkly leotard.

"Her *arabesques* are pretty impressive," Scarlett whispered to Rochelle.

"You're way more talented than she is," Rochelle assured her. "Just wait till I get this boot off. She's no competition for either of us."

The Teen Solos were next, with Addison

leading the pack. She strolled onstage dressed in a black dress, pearl necklace, and sunglasses. She was Audrey Hepburn's character in *Breakfast at Tiffany's*, and she did a sad, haunting ballet to "Moon River."

"Wow," Bria said, watching from the wings. "She's really amazing."

"She's not bad," Liberty said with a sniff. "Where do you suppose Justine stole her from?"

As she walked back to the wings, Addison purposely bumped into Rochelle, knocking one of her crutches out from under her.

"Watch it!" Rochelle yelled, trying to steady herself.

"Sorry," Addison replied. "I forgot we had a little old lady limping around backstage. It's just not safe for you here. Maybe you should go home and take a nap."

Rochelle gritted her teeth. "The only ones going home are you guys . . . empty-handed," she said. "Because the Divas are going to win every title today."

Addison laughed in her face. "I don't think so. Especially when 'Rock' here needs a rocking chair."

"It's not nice to make fun of Rock," Gracie spoke up. "She's hurt."

Addison patted her on the head. "Maybe you could both go and take a nap. Babies need a lot of sleep."

"I am not a baby!" Gracie screamed.

Hayden saw what was happening and rushed to Rochelle's side.

"Is there a problem?" he asked calmly.

"She's being mean to me and Rock," Gracie said, pointing an accusing finger at Addison.

"Aw, I forgot you had a bodyguard to fight your battles for you, Rochelle." Addison smirked.

"I don't need anyone to fight my battles," Rochelle countered. She hoped that didn't hurt Hayden's feelings, but she was not going to let this girl push her around, crutches or no crutches.

"She's right. I'm not fighting anyone's battles," Hayden interrupted. "I'm just sharing a little advice."

"Advice?" Addison laughed. "What advice could *you* possibly give me? I've been competing my whole life."

Hayden ignored her bragging. " 'I do not try to dance better than anyone else. I only try to dance better than myself,' " he said.

Addison looked at him, puzzled.

"What is that supposed to mean?"

"It's a quote from Mikhail Baryshnikov, one of the greatest dancers of all time," Hayden answered.

"Hayden is really smart," Gracie whispered to Rochelle.

"It means you should stop picking on the Divas and worry about your own dancing," he said. "Because trust me . . . you need to worry. I just heard Justine saying that was the sloppiest *chaîné* she'd ever seen."

Addison looked petrified. She scanned the bleachers for her dance coach. "Did she really say that? Or are you making it up?"

Hayden grinned. He waved to no one in the bleachers. "Hey, Justine! Over here! I found Addison for you."

Addison took off without another nasty word.

"Hayden is our hero!" Gracie exclaimed.

"I second that. Thanks for stomping on those Feet," Rochelle added.

"You're welcome," Hayden replied. "No one picks on us Divas."

CHAPTER 14

Dancing in the Rain

Anya was up next—and she was more than a little nervous to be up against her former City Feet teammates.

"They're just waiting for me to mess up," she told Rochelle.

Rochelle knew she wasn't as good at pep talks as Scarlett, but she did her best. "You won't mess up. You're an amazing dancer," she told Anya. "We're so lucky to have you on our team."

Anya took a deep breath. "You mean that? Because I could totally understand if you guys didn't want me. I was with the enemy once, after all. And Mandy, Regan, and Addison are pretty mean to you."

"At first, we didn't want you," Rochelle admitted. "But you've been a real team player. You saved our group dance."

Anya smiled. "Thanks, Rock."

Rochelle adjusted the veil one last time to make sure it was draped down Anya's back. "Now go out there and show them what Divas are made of."

Anya's classical routine was mesmerizing.

"I don't even know what this ballet is about and this dance is making me cry," Bria whispered. "Anya just pours her heart into it."

Rochelle nodded. She watched as Anya stretched her arms to the heavens and twirled effortlessly across the stage *en pointe*. Her face showed pain and anguish—and also hope and faith. She ended—as Rochelle had directed—by picking up the vase and bowing deeply before the audience.

The crowd gave her a standing ovation. Rochelle saw that Toni sat stubbornly in her seat, refusing to rise.

"What's up with that?" Bria asked. "Toni looks mad. Did Anya do something wrong?"

Rochelle gulped. "I think I did. I changed a few details of her dance."

"Rock, you didn't!" Scarlett exclaimed. "You know how much that freaks Toni out!"

"It was for her own good. It didn't make any sense!"

Scarlett shook her head. "It doesn't matter. Never mess with Miss Toni's choreography. No wonder there's steam coming out of her ears."

Rochelle hoped that Hayden's routine would take her teacher's mind off her edited version of Anya's dance. He glided across the stage, smooth as silk, and twirled around the streetlamp before letting go of his umbrella. It floated up, up, up over his head. At least something worked! Then she noticed the umbrella hovering right in front of Hayden's face. The heavy curved handle smacked him several times in the head as he did his *pirou-ettes*.

"Uh-oh," Scarlett said, covering her eyes. "I hope he doesn't get a concussion."

"He better not!" Liberty warned Rochelle. "We have our duet coming up."

At the end of the routine, after beating Hayden up, the umbrella delicately drifted back down to earth.

"I'm so sorry!" Rochelle said, rushing to apologize. "I don't know what happened!"

"I've never had a rumble with an umbrella," he said, rubbing his forehead. He had a huge goose egg that was already turning black and blue. "It packs quite a punch!"

"Here you go," Liberty said sweetly, handing him an ice pack.

Rochelle growled. What else could go wrong today?

CHAPTER 15

Who's Afraid of the Big Bad Wolf?

Rochelle braced herself for the two City Feet duets. She knew Justine would pull out all the stops, and she wasn't the slightest bit surprised when Mandy and Regan walked onstage wearing neon-blue-and-green tuxedos and sunglasses.

"What are they supposed to be?" Liberty cracked. "Disco penguins?"

The music started, and a blast of Korean lyrics filled the gym.

"Oh, no." Bria gulped. "It couldn't be."

Rochelle grabbed the program and read the name of the routine: "Gangnam Style Revisited."

Mandy flipped and flew through the air, while Regan hopped up and down, pumping her fists. The craziest part was when the pair rolled a trampoline onstage and did *grand jetés* six feet in the air! They left the stage to thunderous applause, side-skipping to the sidelines.

"What did you think?" Hayden asked Rochelle.

Rochelle wanted to say she hated it—that it was lame and Mandy and Regan were awful. But she couldn't. The dance was undeniably cool and creative—a modern acro masterpiece.

She thought about how Miss Toni would handle it. How she would motivate the team rather than tell them their chances of topping it were slim to nothing.

"I think you and Liberty have to be even better than they are," she said simply. "And I know you can do it."

Hayden smiled. "I'd feel better if it were you and me going out there. But I'll do my best."

Addison Walsh and Phoebe Malone from City Feet were up next. Rochelle read the title of the routine: "Picnic in the Park" and hoped it would be more mellow than the last duet. But instead, the lights in the gym grew dim and a lone wolf howled over the loudspeaker.

"What in the world is that?" Bria whispered.

"Maybe Mandy turned into a werewolf," Liberty suggested. "I always knew she was a little beast."

Addison leaped onto the stage dressed in a gray furry vest and black unitard. Phoebe skipped in wearing a red hooded cape and carrying a basket.

"It's the Big Bad Wolf and Red Riding Hood," Scarlett said. "I never saw that one coming."

The dance was dark and dangerous, with acro choreography to match. Gracie hid her eyes every time the wolf pounced at Red.

"I hate this story!" she squealed.

"It gave her nightmares when our mom read it to us," Scarlett explained.

Liberty shook her head. "Addison would give anyone nightmares."

Suddenly, Phoebe flipped her hood inside out

and turned it into a superhero cape with a big letter *R* on the back. She took off after Addison, surrounding her with a succession of aerials and somersaults.

"Go, Red Riding Hood!" Gracie yelled. "Get the Big Bad Wolf!"

Liberty covered Gracie's mouth. "No cheering for the enemy."

In the end, the wolf was left cowering in the corner while a triumphant Red did *fouettés* onstage.

"I liked the part where the evil wolf gets her butt kicked." Liberty smirked.

"It was another great routine." Rochelle sighed. "City Feet is going to be tough to beat."

Liberty grabbed Hayden by the arm and pulled him forward. "They haven't seen us yet," she said. "Right, Hayden?"

"Right. I got pounded by an umbrella. I'm not going to take a beating from City Feet, too." Hayden tried his best to sound cool and confident, but Rochelle could tell he was unsure.

"I think City Feet should be very afraid." She smiled. "Their numbers can't compare to ours."

But she crossed her fingers as the stage crew began setting up for the Divas' duet.

Please, she thought, *let this be awesome!*

CHAPTER 16

Love's First Kiss

Hayden waited with Liberty while the school custodian climbed up the ladder to secure their white curtain panels to the ceiling.

"When I say 'lights down,' go dark," Rochelle instructed the person running the light board. "Got it? Then you shine the white spotlight right in the middle behind the curtains, so we see them in shadow."

He nodded. "I got it."

Rochelle limped over to the sidelines and hoped for the best. It was now out of her hands.

As the first bars of music began to play, Rochelle

signaled for the lights to dim. She cued the spot-light and the wind machine. Liberty and Hayden appeared as ghostly shadows against the white, flowing curtains. The audience oohed and aahed. It was magical. It was perfect. Rochelle just wished that the duet was hers.

As the crowd cheered, Liberty curtsied a dozen times and blew kisses. There was no arguing that she and Hayden were an amazing pair.

"You did it," Rochelle told them. "Great job."

"And you did it," he corrected her. "You made that number run smoothly. It would have been a disaster without your direction. We would have been stumbling around in the dark."

"I agree," Toni said. For the first time that entire day, she actually had a smile on her face. "The duet was everything I imagined it to be. Just beautiful."

Rochelle let out a huge sigh of relief. She had done *something* right.

The only thing she had left to worry about was the group dance. "We have a two-hour break. I want to run it as many times as we can," Toni told them.

"Ugh," Liberty complained. "We know that dance backward, forward, and upside down! What could possibly go wrong?"

Rochelle didn't want to try and guess. "You know what my mom always says," she told Scarlett. "When it rains, it pours."

The girls found a quiet classroom to use as a studio. They pushed the desks and chairs back against the walls and took their places. Rochelle hit a button on her MP3 player and the sound track filled the air.

Toni watched with a critical eye, correcting every bent knee, slouchy shoulder, and sickled foot. Rochelle circled around the group, making sure everyone started on the same count of the music.

"What do you think?" Toni asked her. "Are they ready?"

The last thing Rochelle wanted to do was diss her Diva-mates. But there were a few things that still seemed off. She owed it to them to be honest.

"Bria and Gracie were a beat behind on the entrance. And Scarlett, your *assemblé* could be sharper."

She then turned to Liberty. "You could get a little more extension on your *arabesque*."

"What? It was perfect!" Liberty started to argue.

"I think those are very good notes," Toni said, stopping her. "I agree with Rochelle one hundred percent. Anything else you'd like to add?"

Rochelle thought for a moment. "I just want to say that you've all worked so hard and no matter who wins or loses today, you should be really proud of yourselves."

Toni smiled. "I couldn't have said it better myself. Except for the winning or losing part. You'd better win."

CHAPTER 17

Making a Splash

The Divas watched anxiously as the other teams performed. There were several good routines (Top Toes from L.A. did a salute to Hollywood, including an acro routine across the Walk of Fame) and a few bizarre ones (Candy Corns from Iowa were scarecrows tapping through the cornfields).

"The waiting is the worst part," Anya said. "I just want to get it over with!"

"At least we're up before City Feet," Liberty added. "Let them sweat a little longer."

Finally, the announcer summoned them to the stage: "Performing a contemporary dance titled 'After the Storm,' please welcome Dance Divas."

Rochelle cued the sound track, and a bolt of lightning crackled across the back gymnasium wall. The wind machine started to whip, and a curtain of rain poured down as the music pulsed and the thunder boomed. The girls made their way across the floor, helping one another through the devastating hurricane. Scarlett, Liberty, and Anya spun in *pirouettes*, as if the wind was propelling them. Bria rolled across the floor, arching her back and reaching for the heavens, pleading with them to stop the destruction and despair. Gracie's part was the most emotional: a little child, lost and searching high and low for her mother. She walked across the floor in a perfect handstand, finally settling in a pile of newspaper that she draped over her head as shelter. Suddenly, the rain stopped and a ray of sunlight broke through, shining down on the dancers. They took one another's hands and stood tall onstage. They shed their ragged, dirty skirts and shawls to reveal spotless white leotards. Finally, Gracie held up a newspaper with the headline: REBUILD, RESTORE, RENEW.

The crowd went wild. There wasn't a dry eye in the gymnasium. The judges were passing around a box of tissues.

The girls raced offstage to hug Rochelle.

"That was amazing!" Scarlett congratulated her. "Absolutely amazing!"

"A first-place winner if I ever saw one," Toni agreed.

"Don't count on that," Justine said, walking over to them. "That was an amazing number. I give credit where credit is due. But you haven't seen ours yet."

Rochelle checked the program. The name of City Feet's routine was "Puzzlement."

"What do you suppose that means?" she asked her teammates.

"It means Justine didn't want anyone to know what she was up to," Liberty said.

As the announcer called them to the stage, the City Feet team girls strutted out wearing black robes.

"What the heck?" Bria asked. "Are they supposed to be monks?"

"Let's hope Mandy takes a vow of silence," Scarlett said, laughing.

A strange, eerie tune began playing over the speakers. It had bells, whistles, and odd chanting. Rochelle strained her ears to make out the words. "I think they're backward . . . ," she said. There were strange sounds of a record skipping and scratching.

Just then, the dancers unwrapped their robes. They were dressed in black-and-white-checkered bodysuits resembling the squares of a crossword puzzle. They twisted themselves in odd shapes, as Mandy flipped and twirled around them. Random letters and numbers appeared on the walls and ceiling. It was dizzying.

"This is pazy . . . and not in a good way," Gracie interjected.

"You can say that again," Hayden spoke up. "I can't figure it out."

"I think that's the point," Toni suggested. "Justine is trying to make a statement about the uncertainty of life."

"You get that . . . from that?" Rochelle said. "All I'm getting is motion sickness."

"I know my frenemy. She likes to push the envelope and make the judges think. I can't say that I hate it . . ."

"I can," Liberty said. "And I think the audience does, too." When the music ended, no one knew if the routine was over and whether or not to clap.

"It doesn't matter what the audience thinks; it's how the judges will judge it," Toni replied. "It was very inventive and edgy. I think they might have a good chance of taking first place."

CHAPTER 18

Trophy Time

It took the judges over an hour to deliberate on all the divisions.

Petite Solo was the first to be announced. "In second place, Mandy Hammond from City Feet with 'Red, Red Robin.'"

"Oh, my gooshness." Gracie squeezed Hayden's hand as the Divas huddled on the floor. "Do you think? Could it be?"

"In first place, Gracie Borden from Dance Divas with 'Cooking by the Book'!"

Gracie jumped up and down. "I won! I won! I won!" she screamed.

"See? And you were worried about the pancake-turned-UFO," Hayden said to Rochelle teasingly.

Gracie beamed and made sure that Mandy got a good look at her winning trophy. It was so tall and heavy, she could barely lift it. "It's bigger than yours," she said to Mandy. "So there!"

Anya got first place for Teen Solo, while Hayden came in third runner-up. Rochelle felt terrible; the in-your-face umbrella had been totally her fault.

"You win some, you lose some," he reassured her.

"Don't let Toni hear you say that," Bria warned him. "She doesn't like to lose. Ever."

When the announcer said Hayden and Liberty won for Best Duet, Rochelle's heart sunk, just a little. She was thrilled for him, but jealous that he and Liberty shared something they never would.

"Look on the bright side," Scarlett said, trying to distract her. "Mandy and Regan came in third, and Addison and Phoebe were second. Justine must be freaking out."

But not even City Feet's defeat could make her feel better. Rochelle watched as Hayden and Liberty posed for pictures with their arms around each other. Rochelle shut her eyes tight; it hurt too much to think of him with another girl.

"Hey, you taking a nap?" Hayden whispered, sitting back down beside her.

"No. I just . . . I got something in my eye."

"Oh. Let me check . . ." Hayden leaned in closer. "I don't see anything." Then he planted a kiss on her cheek. Rochelle blushed.

"Next time, that title is ours," he said.

Rochelle hoped there would be a next time. She wasn't sure Miss Toni would ever forgive her for all of today's fiascos. She was trying to put them out of her head when she felt a drop of water land on it. Then another. Then another.

She held out her hand. "Is it me, or is it raining in here?" she asked.

Hayden looked up. "I think the PVC pipe is leaking."

"I'm getting drizzled on," Scarlett whispered. "What's going on?"

Before they could investigate further, the announcer took his position at the microphone.

"Our final category is Best Junior Group Performance," he said. He read several other studio names, till he reached first runner-up.

"Wow, this was a close one. Only one-tenth of a point separates our overall winner and the first runner-up." The Divas all joined hands and waited for the names to be called. Rochelle wiped a few more water drops off her face. *Hurry up!* She silently willed the host to read the results. *I'm getting drenched!*

"First runner-up, 'After the Storm,' Dance Divas, New Jersey . . ."

Rochelle was stunned. They'd lost to City Feet!

Mandy, Regan, Addison, Phoebe, and the rest of the City Feet team raced up to retrieve their trophy. Justine joined them onstage, beaming. She even had an acceptance speech prepared. "We just want to say a big thank-you to the judges and congratulate our competitors," she said. "Toni and Dance Divas, especially. Good try, girls!"

All of a sudden, water burst through a section of the pipe. It poured down right on the spot where Justine and her team were standing as they posed for pictures, soaking them from head to toe.

"Help! I can't swim!" Mandy whimpered.

"Awesome!" Hayden laughed. "We flooded the Feet!"

"Rock, did you plan that?" Scarlett whispered.

"I wish!" she said, cracking up. "Liberty?"

"Nuh-uh," she answered. "This was a natural disaster."

Even Miss Toni couldn't help laughing. "Aw, poor Justine. Looks like the Divas rained on your parade."

"You're not mad that they beat us?" Rochelle asked her.

"Mad? No. Disappointed? Sure. But seeing Justine doused makes up for it a little." She winked.

CHAPTER 19

The Return of Rock

Rochelle didn't think the four weeks of being "benched" from the Divas would ever be over—or that she would miss the endless dance drills and Miss Toni's constant correcting. But when the doctor finally gave her the okay, she couldn't wait to be back in the studio again.

"Welcome back!" Scarlett cheered. She'd hung a banner across Rochelle's locker in the dressing room and baked her M&M's brownies. "We missed you!"

"The Rock returns!" Bria said, hugging her.

Even Liberty seemed relieved to see her. "Miss

Toni says she wants to choreograph another duet with Hayden for next month's Ovation competition. You ready to pick up where we left off?"

Rochelle remembered the story Toni told her about Marcus. Instead of being jealous, Rochelle told her teammate, "You go ahead and do the duet. I'd rather be Swanilda."

"Huh?" Liberty scratched her head. "I don't get it. I thought you liked Hayden."

"I do," Rochelle said. "And he likes me. So I'm fine with you dancing with him. Really."

It felt amazing to be back in the studio. After her clunky boot, even her toe shoes felt comfy. She stood at the *barre*, waiting for Miss Toni to direct her.

Instead, her coach took a seat on a stool at the front of the studio. "Divas, we're growing—and I don't just mean in size." She looked at Anya and Hayden. "I think Leaps and Bounds was just the beginning."

Rochelle certainly felt like she'd changed over the past few months. She was more certain of her footing on and off the stage, and she understood much better why Toni did what she did—and that trying to fill her shoes was impossible. Yes, her teacher was tough and strict, but that's what a great dance team needed in a leader. She made herself a promise that from now on, she'd try to be on time to class and not give Toni such a hard time.

Liberty raised her hand. "Um, Miss Toni, what do you mean 'the beginning'? The beginning of what?"

Toni smiled. "I think we've turned a corner. I'm ready to shake things up, and I think you guys can handle it."

Hayden glanced over at Rochelle and mouthed, "Help." Bria looked like she was going to be sick. But Rochelle wasn't the least bit nervous. Rain, wind, sleet—even City Feet—couldn't stop the Dance Divas!

Glossary of Dance Terms

Arabesque: a move where the dancer stands on one leg with the other leg extended behind her at 90 degrees.

Assemblé: a jump from one to both feet—usually landing in fifth position.

Cabriole: a scissorlike leap in the air, with one leg outstretched and the other beating against it.

Chaîné: a series of quick turns.

Chassé: a step in which one foot chases the other foot out of its position.

Echappé sauté: a deep plié followed by a jump; the legs "escape."

Fouetté: a turning step where the leg whips out to the side.

Grand jeté: a large forward leap in the air that looks like a flying split.

Pas de deux: a duet.

Paso doble: means "two steps" in Spanish because of the marchlike movements. This is a dance where the man and woman play the bullfighter and his cape or bullfighter and bull.

Piqué turn: a traveling turning step on one leg.

Pirouette: a turn on one leg with the other leg behind.

Plié: a bend of the knees with hips, legs, and feet turned out.

Port de bras: graceful movements of the arms.

Promenade en arabesque: a pivot turn on the standing foot with the other foot extended behind in arabesque position.

Relevé: to rise up on pointe or on demi-pointe.

Rond de jambe: a move where the dancer makes half circles with one leg.

Salsa: a contemporary Latin dance.

Saut de basque: a traveling step where the dancer turns in the air with one foot brought up to the knee of the other leg.

Tour jeté: the dancer leaps from one foot, makes a half turn in the air, and lands on the other foot.

Sheryl Berk is a proud ballet mom and a *New York Times* bestselling author. She has collaborated with numerous celebrities on their memoirs, including Britney Spears, *Glee*'s Jenna Ushkowitz, and *Shake It Up*'s Zendaya. Her book with Bethany Hamilton, *Soul Surfer*, hit #1 on the *New York Times* bestseller list and became a major motion picture. She is also the author of The Cupcake Club book series with her ten-year-old daughter, Carrie.